Transfixed

Fated Choices Book #1

Bella Rose

Author's Note

Transfixed has taken at least 10 years to find its way into the world.

I always said I would write a book one day and I hope that you enjoy it, now that it is here.

Transfixed is essentially an opening scene to a much larger story and I for one am looking forward to the ride.

If you'd like to follow me I can be found in the following places:

www.facebook.com/bellaroseuk
www.twitter.com/bellarosewriter
www.overtheultravioletrainbow.uk

Dear Reader,

I hear things! Things I have no business hearing and it has defined the course of my life. Sometimes I believe that I was chosen for this life to serve some purpose and achieve some good. Other times I KNOW, without a shadow of a doubt, that I was cursed into this existence for reasons that I cannot fathom.

My earliest memories are lost to the haze and an all-consuming rage. I have no clear recollections, only a vague sense of danger and a deep insatiable need, but even then, my 'talent' makes it impossible to truly know if these are my memories or somebody else's.

Just to explain when I say I hear things, I don't mean that I hear actual sounds with my ears, I am referring to thoughts and feelings. Sometimes, it's like overhearing somebody have a conversation with themselves when they think no one is around. More often it is a vague sense of intention or emotion. Sometimes I see flashes of colour, or smell something that triggers a mental response. Other times, it is exactly like watching a horror movie, those thoughts I get loud and clear, sometimes it's almost three-dimensional. I suppose that's a good thing, it makes my choices easier.

I see the Darkness so clearly that I am able to shy from the Light.

I suppose that's where this whole thing starts, well not really, as I said, most of my earliest memories are lost to the haze of time. But, I guess, this particular chapter of my existence really starts with hearing things. The night was like any other, I heard and I followed. I took what was mine to take and saved what was in danger of ending. But Light crossed my path that night and my journey skewed off into the mist, and for the first time in literally forever, I had no clue where to step next. I just knew that every step was somehow vital to my continued existence. So it was, that with some trepidation, I set one foot in front of the other, to face what seemed to be a saga of almost 'Fated Choices.'

Jenna

1

Chasing Darkness

Jenna

I wake, as usual, and catch the tail end of an image so full of Darkness, I have a hard time imagining this being living in the same city as me and our paths not crossing before. The man is a predator to his very core but not for much longer. Once I've caught your Darkness, you can be sure that the clock is ticking. I usually like to be positive by following, and intervening at the last possible moment, just for my own clear conscience really. If I must walk this road, then I do at least like to pretend to do some good while I'm traveling.

He is thinking about a time before and how he'd enjoyed her screams and cries to "Please stop" and "Don't do this." "Robbie. No, Please Stop, Please?" Her muffled cries ran through my head, as I see through his eyes, the horror on her face. She already knew he wouldn't stop, but she kept on fighting and trying to push him away. Unfortunately, he loved it when they fight and it spurred him on. It really is the weirdest sensation, to feel his excitement and my own disgust at the same time. His enthusiasm to keep her pinned down had pushed him to squeeze harder than usual, and he had accidentally choked her to death. That had been the first life he'd taken, but it was certainly not the most recent. His games have taken on a new dimension since that night, and he has had to keep moving to remain undetected.

I realize that is why he has not crossed my path before now, he's been moving around the country, looking for his thrills, but this is home ground, the city where his first body lay. That's why he recalls her with such clarity tonight, it is like walking down a particularly fond memory lane for him, and I have the damned privilege of walking it with him.

"Damn you to the Seven Shades of Hell, Robbie," I said out loud as I rise from the bed. Might as well get on with it!

I could see from Robbie's head that he is hitting the club scene tonight, and so I dress accordingly. Not that getting in would be a problem, but one really should make an effort when out for the evening, don't you think?

Usually I follow fairly close behind my mark, but he's broadcasting so loudly, that it's like a siren call to me. For that reason alone, I think I would be inclined to see his reign of terror end, just so I can get some peace again. Once I have heard your Darkness, I don't seem to be able to 'unhear' it. It has to be silenced, or I will always know where you are. As a result, my chase is usually a foregone conclusion, almost to the point of being tedious sometimes.

These killers and rapists, you'd think they would be a bit more impulsive, or at least passionate about their chosen hobby. Apparently there are geeks in all walks of life. These dark seeds are just as anal about their system or procedure as any techno geek anywhere.

I watch as Robbie joins a gaggle of girls near the front of the queue. He seems to know them, or at least convinces them that they know him, and they escort him into the club without the security guards paying much attention. He's good, I'll give him that. His powers of persuasion however, I am certain, are nothing compared to mine.

I am trying to decide whether to take the front door, or the fire exit, when I smell something that wakes a deep longing inside me, it's almost like a feeling of...of well.... Home, really, like safety and warmth rolled into one. What the hell? I'm a bit thrown by this as I have no memories of feeling anything like it before. I feel safe and warm, comforted as though I am not perched on a rooftop in the middle of the city. The sharp cold gust of a south-easterly wind releases me from my reverie, and I quickly drop to ground level before it can grip me again.

My true eyes are a little too obviously supernatural for

your standard grade human, and so I must glamour them for every interaction.

Since I'm still slightly confused by the scent I caught on the roof, I decide that the fire exit will be a better choice, once I'm inside, my eyes won't matter.

I snap the handle from the door and it swings open towards me, bringing with it that special blend of nightclub smells. Alcohol in varying degrees of both sweet and sharp, there's always vomit towards the end of the night, and the sickly stench of desperation, suffocating amounts of desperation. Nightclubs can be quite overwhelming generally, but with senses as heightened as mine, it can be almost disabling. I survey the scene in front of me as I acclimatize.

This modern music always strikes me as being mostly just noise with very little rhythm or melody. The underlying beat seems to control the rhythm of every human heart in the room, and I wonder how many suffer medical problems as a result. To me, the pounding bass is like an earth deep reverberation that rings through the whole building and each individual item or person inside.

There are over two hundred human hearts beating in a coordinated rhythm inside this building, and right now they are combining to overwhelm my willpower. I have to lock down nearly all of my baser instincts with an iron fist. Increasing my 'get the hell away from me' glamour, I cast my eyes over the wall of sweaty, gyrating bodies in front of me.

TRANSFIXED

The electronic lights flash and spin, creating and eliminating shadows in mere seconds. The dance room itself is designed to look like some kind of dungeon, I think, since there are shackles on the wall with ominous skeletons dangling freely. I wonder again at my self-imposed mission to extinguish the Darkness, considering the very evident depravity of the human race symbolized in this room. I stay to the edge for a while, letting the music move through me, watching the movie in my head as my mark zeroes in on his chosen target.

I have my eyes closed now, but I can feel someone watching me and there's that feeling again of comfort and safety. I have never felt anything like it in all my years. Opening my eyes, I spot him. He's young, a mere child really, compared to me anyway, but there's something there, in his eyes, that reaches for me on some instinctive level.

The boy...man...is staring at me as though he can't turn away. My own gaze is locked now onto his piercing blue eyes and I feel drawn, like a moth to a flame. I can see and feel the very Lightness of his soul. Planting my feet solidly, I almost groan aloud when he steps forward, moving almost unconsciously into my space. He leans forward as though to speak intimately with me.

I step sideways and away in a mild panic, my control is good...but...there is just something...

Raising an eyebrow I say, "Keep moving, Boy Scout, you're not my type!"

"Why?" he asks me, like we're about to debate something earth-shattering, and I can't help but laugh. Shaking my head, I look him over and wish very briefly that I sometimes played in the Light. "Get away from me–Immediately!" I spit at him, as it dawns on me that he is what I've been smelling, that safe, homey, comfort smell that's messing with me tonight is him.

As I stalk away, he says, "I'm Luc, by the way. Hope to see you around."

"I know." I can't help but sigh. "But I'm leaving now. I've found my date."

Robbie is chatting to a girl-woman, who seems for all the world as though her aim in life is to emulate one of those children's toys. You know; the ones that make women seem like plastic idiots with big boobs and zero intelligence? She is perched, teetering on the edge of a large cauldron in the centre of the room, which is belching smoke onto the dance floor. Zeroing in, I get a clear read of his intentions as he's persuading her to join him for a 'walk.' I move into the scene as though passing and divert his attention, pressing my body to his.

A little glamour convinces him that he has been chatting to me the whole time, and we move out through the club. As we manoeuvre through the front doors, he steps ahead and in the lead, taking my hand and steering me away from the crowd waiting out front. Robbie leads me along cobblestone streets, which without my superior balance might have been a problem in these boots. As it gets quieter, he pulls me closer and starts in with his silver-tongued patter that has clearly worked well in the past. I honestly do wonder how some of these girls survive into their twenties, if they believe all the rubbish spouted by such boys, but I digress.

I allow Robbie to steer me into an alleyway, as is his plan, and within minutes he's attempting to undress me. Now don't get me wrong, I look good and I dress well. I quite like these denim-look leggings that are all the fashion at the moment. Anyway, with my ankle boot heels and blue denim jacket, over black vest top, I am quite a striking figure—— especially if you catch sight of my true eyes. Even so, to be this desperate to undress me, he must really get a kick from his little hobby; it's almost like he's desperate for a hit of something.

I'm about to move into hunt mode, when I smell home again, quickly followed by... "Hey, take your damn hands of her!" It's the guy from the club, Luc. Is he following me?

"I said leave her alone, can't you see she's not interested?" Suddenly they are both looking at me, as though I have sprouted a third eye, and I realize a little too late that Robbie is confused. The glamour has worn off, and I look nothing like the girl he picked out. Luc looks unsure because I clearly don't appear to be relieved enough, having been rescued in such a brave manner. To be fair, I'm struggling to even look upset at the molestation I've endured up to this point. I simply can't grasp what this guy is doing here, or why my head is so messed up. What the hell is wrong with me?

"Yeah, err sorry, babe. I guess I got the wrong end of the stick. I'll see you around," Robbie mumbles, as he staggers away, intending to go home to bed. I seem to have overdosed him a little. I didn't even realize that was a thing, to be honest, my marks don't usually walk away from me.

I turn to Luc, who now seems unsure if I wanted saving or not, indeed, he seems almost like he's now too shy to ask me. I quickly decide that anyone who scrambles my instincts this much is a bad idea and take a defensive stance. "What in the Seven Shades of Hell are you doing following me down an alleyway? Don't you know there's all sorts of weirdos about? You could have gotten yourself killed!" I yell, wait! What? That's not what I meant to say at all.

Luc looks rather surprised at my choice of words, too, and has no answer, other than to shrug and look sheepish. Staring down at his shoes, he starts to blush. Blush. I mean seriously! The guy just barged into a potential fight for my honour, and now he's blushing and mumbling like a school kid and...for some reason, I'm finding it all rather endearing, like he's a particularly cute puppy. I have got to get the hell away from here.

"Can I like...buy you a coffee or something? I'm a little worried that you haven't realized yet, what just happened...?" He looks up at me, hands down deep in his pockets, and unadulterated hope in his eyes. I find my hands twitching with a need to touch. I want to run my fingers through his messy dark blond hair, and I have to lock myself down, before something terrible happens. To me, or to him, or to the world at large? I really don't know, but I feel like the world is tilting and this really can't be good.

Can I faint? No, I really doubt that. "Look, loser, I don't know what your deal is, but NO I do not want a coffee. Goodnight!" With that I turn on my heel and stride to the end of the alleyway, just in time to run straight into Luc's group of friends, who seem to assume we had been together and start whistling and cat calling. To his credit, as I keep walking, I hear Luc trying to set the record straight, but I don't think they want to believe him.

Jenna

Back at home I'm in a muddle. My aborted hunt and run-in with Luc has left me hungry, confused, and with a head full of Robbie's most sordid memories and fantasies. I'm pacing my apartment like a caged tiger. I don't want him in my head, but can I just follow him home? It's not like there's any doubt who or what he is. I know that I am trying to convince myself that it's fine. I am really not even sure why it's so important to me, it's just the way I deal with the hand I have been dealt. I can't change what I am, but I do have the power to decide WHO I am.

Deciding to only destroy Darkness is a choice I made long ago, it helps me live with the consequences of what I am. I don't even clearly remember the thought process that brought me to this point. I just remember deciding and feeling better for the decision.

I'm starting to convince myself when I feel a different rhythm click into Robbie's brain. He's getting up and going out again, it would seem. This is of course not good for the local girls but fantastic for me. I can round out my evening, as planned, and rid the world of another monster. Oh, the irony.

I follow Robbie to a different club, this time. This one has styled itself after a dark enchanted forest, with shaded corners and private nooks that can be used by couples and predators alike. I suspect an actual dark forest would smell more of mould than the sex and alcohol I can smell here, and really? Fabric Leaves?

He's moving quickly, looking for someone, anyone, I think to begin with, and then I realize he's looking for a girl that reminds him of the first one. He wants to recreate the memory. After about twenty minutes, he seems to settle for a shy-looking girl, who looks flattered that anyone would talk to her, perfect victim material, really. She looks so grateful to be the focus of his attention and so I try to view him as she clearly does. Charming? I suppose so, it all sounds very good, I guess. It's just that I've been around a while and have heard it all before. Good-looking? Well again, yes, I suppose so in a dark, swarthy kind of way.

I stop to think when the last time was, that I actually

looked at someone and thought them attractive. I continue to ponder this question, even though my brain answered immediately with a nod at Luc–so not going there! I realize that I've tuned Robbie out while I was thinking. I assumed he was going to invite missy outside, but as her panic reaches out to me, I realize he's going to do it right here in the club.

He has ensconced them into one of the many nooks and cubbyholes dotted around, and I am instantly aware that, only I know what is going on. I need to move fast if I want to intervene. I don't really have time to be subtle, and I catch him around the throat, lifting him off his feet. He looks stunned and then does a double take. "You! Did you drug me earlier? I have the worst hangover, bitch!" I just look at him, amazed that this predatory man has the nerve to be insulted by the idea that I may have taken advantage of him.

With that my anger flares and my eyes burn crimson for a second. He pales and tries to shrink out of my hold, which ticks all my boxes. I'm getting a reaction and he looks like he might actually piss himself. "Are you going to kill me?" he squeaks. I just smile, allowing my fangs to drop into sight for the first time tonight; he tries to swallow and fails, since I still have him pinned by the throat. "Why me?" he stammers through his growing fear.

I nod to the girl, she's huddled into herself and she's shaking, either because I've scared her or from the adrenalin run off caused by thinking Robbie would rape her. "For her," I tell him. "And all of her sisters!"

He seems to understand that I am his judge, jury, and executioner and that there is nothing he can do about it. "Will it hurt?" he asks me, in an almost detached way

"Oh yes, my Darkness. I will allow you no mercies." With that, I cover his mouth with my other hand and bite down hard.

2

Feeding

Jenna

It's hard to describe what it's like to feed on the Darkness. I can't compare it to Light food, since I have abstained for so long. Unlike almost everyone else, I know who just vamps it up and is unnecessarily cruel. They don't seem to care about being better, they just 'play.' Apparently, the world is ours to play with and I should 'lighten up,' oh ha-ha.

To feed on the Darkness is to bring an end to just a small part of the evil in this world, allowing the Light just a wee bit more freedom. I like to think that maybe when my time is done here, that my fight against the Darkness will count for something, maybe make my own soul slightly less stained.

I feed from Robbie quickly as he struggles against my hold, but within a few minutes his time is done. I should not have done this here, but he started it by attacking the girl. I drop him to the ground, deciding to leave him, just this once. This is a rather conveniently hidden corner, after all, and it seems fitting to me that Robbie's end should be remembered this way, after the blatant disregard he has demonstrated for his previous victims.

I squat down in front of the girl. "Honey, what's your name?"

"Abigail," she tells me, quiet as a mouse, whilst all the time shaking so violently I am certain that her head will pop off at any moment.

"Abigail, honey, look at me," I instruct her and touch her chin to guide her movement. As soon as I catch her eye, I let my own eyes flash, erasing her fear and memory of the last few minutes. She blinks and stares at me blankly. "Abigail, honey, are you feeling okay?" She looks down and blinks.

"What happened?"

"I think you slipped, hon, maybe bumped your head, you don't remember?"

Abigail looks around confused and then gets to her feet. "Actually, my head does hurt, maybe I'll get a cab and go home?" She makes it sound like a question and she looks at me for approval.

"I think that's probably a good idea, let me help you outside, and see you into a cab."

We step over Robbie and Abigail doesn't even glance at him. At the front of the building, I put Abigail into a taxi and pay the driver, after giving him the address that had helpfully flashed into her mind at the mention of home.

Hopefully tomorrow, she'll wake up groggy and assume that my suggestion of her falling down was correct. I go to leave, and as I look up, I realize I have an audience. Across the street to my right is Anthony, who is looking at me like he wants to beat me into submission, but can't, because he knows I'd leave him where I found him. Also, his boss would not be impressed. Across the street, and to my left, are Luc and his friends; he's staring at me like a dying man in the desert and trying to catch my attention, without alerting his friends. I know instantaneously that I do NOT want these two boys to meet, because Luc must be protected and he's mine to protect. Where that thought comes from I don't know, but there it is.

So I do the only thing I can. I turn and walk away, down the alleyway behind me. As soon as I hit the shadows, I jump, quickly scaling the side of the club like it is a slight hill. Knowing that Anthony will see me go and likely follow, but that to Luc it will simply look as though I have disappeared. I continue to the roof, orienting myself before heading out of the city centre.

3

Summoned

Working my way across the rooftops, I make my way 'home' to the apartment I keep here. It has one of those new-fangled panic rooms, so should I need to, I can spend a day here, but I prefer to head back out to my secluded cottage when I can. No way am I leading Anthony there.

He dropped onto the balcony behind me as I was flicking on the lights and stood lounging in the open French doors, as though he had every right in the world to be there.

"Was there something you wanted, Anthony?" I ask, turning around.

"Is that an offer, princess?"

"Don't call me that!" I snap back, he knows how much

I hate it.

Anthony bows as sarcastically as possible "You are bid, please return home, princess." He smirks up at me.

"It is not MY home, Anthony!"

"In that case, you are bid please visit––immediately." It doesn't look like I have much of a choice, if I am being summoned, then my choices are to either allow Anthony to escort me now, or to be forced later when he returns with his goon squad. I'll be damned, if I am going to make his job easier for him.

Anthony is nothing more than an empty-headed gofer. If I am completely honest, I have more respect for the cretins on which I choose to prey than I do for Anthony. He scurries around, full of his own self-importance, running errands for Marcus and thanking him profusely for the privilege of licking his boots––figuratively or literally, I couldn't care less.

Ignoring Anthony, for the moment, I flop down onto the sofa and consider kicking my boots off. If this degenerates into a fight then I will probably benefit from wearing them. On the whole, they are one of my favourite pairs, and I don't want them ruined when Anthony bleeds on them.

We vampires don't leak particularly easily, but when we do, things tend to get ruined and need burning. Unfortunately, Anthony seems to assume that my footwear removal is a subtle invitation to get comfortable. As I turn to my left, to stretch out with my feet up on the seat, I find myself about to lay them into his lap. Anthony looks mighty pleased with his small victory and smiles in response to my scowl.

In the blink of an eye, Anthony lays his left arm across my ankles effectively pinning my legs in place. He turns towards me, right arm across the back of the sofa. To the casual observer, we would look for all the world like a couple just in from a night out on the town––not that you get many casual observers on the fifth floor, but you catch my drift.

Anthony's eyes glaze slightly, as he allows them to roam my body freely. He leans forward slowly, which allows him to both increase his hold on my ankles and slide his hand up towards my ass at the same time. I know my eyes must be turning red because my vision certainly is, that he would dare lay hands on me.

"What's it to be, princess?" he drawls, enjoying himself "You gonna play nicely with me now, like a good little royal piece of ass? Or shall I fetch the boys and we can force you to comply? Rough it up a little? I bet you'd enjoy..."

Anthony's eyes widen as the crack of his jawbone fills the room. The cut glass ashtray from the coffee table, that I have hit him with, has completely shattered between the combined force of his jaw and my right hand. The pieces of glass cascade between us, as though he were showering me with diamonds instead of insinuating that I should entertain him and his cronies. He sits up, still confused, and assesses the damage to his face. Obviously, I take the opportunity to regain my feet and illustrate my anger further with a solid right hook to his nose, which makes a satisfying crunch.

My monster rouses with the unexpected violence and I get in Anthony's face, full of primal fury.

"You will NOT touch me again, or I promise, you WILL lose both hands––Permanently! Do you understand?" I am gripping his neck now, beneath his jawline, and as my nails dig into his throat, close to his jugular, he makes an involuntary whimper and nods minutely. I stare into his eyes a few seconds longer to impress my point, and I can see my own crimson irises staring back at me.

My monster is now fully aroused, and I have an almost overwhelming desire to bleed Anthony, simply because I can. I am teetering right on the very brink of the Darkness. Anthony must sense my struggle for control, because he closes his eyes and seems to almost diminish beneath my hand. I feel him mentally withdraw from the confrontation, and my monster crows in her victory. Her hold over me eases slightly with her jubilation, and it is just enough for me to regain control. I push Anthony from me with force. I am vaguely aware that he has crashed into, and probably broken my furniture, as I turn and stalk into the bathroom, almost taking the door off its hinges as I slam it closed behind me.

Leaning on the sink for support, I stare at myself in the mirror and take deep, deliberate, and totally unnecessary breaths, as I watch the red fade from my eyes to be replaced by my usual iridescent violet. "What the actual... Eurgh!" I groan out loud. What was he thinking, he can't have honestly assumed I would ignore a threat like that? It vaguely occurs to me that he may consider this to be a joke; he does have a peculiar sense of humour; empty-headed reject!

I can hear Anthony moving about in the next room and realize I have a decision to make. Either go now and see what Marcus deems important enough to summon me in such a way. Or I can force a second confrontation with Anthony, when he has backup and will more fiercely defend his wounded pride.

I have no real concerns that I can't hold my own, but truly, it probably isn't worth the effort. Besides a few days in France might help get the Boy Scout from the club out of my head.

Decided, I wash Anthony's blood from my hands and straighten up. Biker boots will be better in the snow I think, I would hate to ruin suede after all.

4

Chateau de la Mothe-Chandeniers

Jenna

As the carriage draws along the driveway, I remember the last time I left this place. I hate returning and this occasion feels no less painful than the last. Anthony is flopped listlessly across from me, pretending to not be watching my chest. Equally, I sit looking out the window and pretend not to notice his ogling. Physically, he'd been nothing but a gentleman since we left the apartment. Not even complaining about the pain of his healing jaw, or broken nose, or indeed the fact that his spilled blood has ruined the rather expensive coat he'd been wearing. There was snow on the ground that looked to be about ten inches deep. As much as I hate this place, it does look beautiful in the snow. In 1932, this building was destroyed in a fire that was apparently started whilst the then owner was having a central heating system installed––Oops.

After its destruction it was left to rot, and as far as most of the world is concerned it is still rotting now. Actually, it's glamoured to look derelict and abandoned; you can only see it's restored beauty if you're allowed to. The castle is surrounded by an honest to goodness moat and can only be reached via its single bridge, which of course is rigged to drop into the moat should the castle be attacked; all very medieval.

The carriage eventually pulls to a stop at the front steps. I step down into the snow cleared courtyard, ascending the steps as Anthony saunters off, with a cat that ate the cream expression.

"Good evening, Madam, may I take your coat?"

"Henry, please don't defer to me in this way. You know I dislike it."

"And you know that I must or be punished, Madam," he replies, tilting his head and giving me a knowing look. I sigh theatrically as I hand him my coat. Henry smiles and asks after my luggage.

"I didn't bring anything, dear boy, I am NOT staying."

"Ah, well then your room is ready. I imagine I shall be instructed to find clothing for you, since I believe Sir intends for you to stay at least this week. Also, Madam, I would imagine that you would rather not spend any length of time wearing that particular top...?" Henry gestures to the vest top and jacket I had kept on under my heavier coat, only now realizing I was spattered in gore from my altercation with Anthony.

Henry bows and backs away, knowing quite well that I was attempting to gain control of my temper. Sir knows, quite well, that I hate it here with its parties, politics, and bullshit. I must remember to thank Henry later for giving me fair warning so that I might retain my control later, when I am summoned.

Marcus

I watch from above as Jenna and Anthony enter the chateau. She is, of course, as beautiful as ever with her raven hair and striking cheekbones. Never before have I seen eyes like Jenna's, they positively glow in the dark and could surely transfix any passing soul. That she would choose to prey only on the murderers and rapists of the world has ever confused and annoyed me. Such a beauty should be here, at my beck and call. Yet, after all this time, she refuses to heel.

Soon, I had been assured, the time would come when the true king and queen would rule the supernatural world. I am positive that I must be this foretold king, just as I am certain that Jenna must be the queen. Only that could account for her strength, both physical and mental. Who else could resist feeding from the Light when surrounded perpetually in such Darkness? Still she shines, almost like a beacon.

Jenna inspires loyalty in the most unlikely places. Even now, knowing that his master is most certainly watching, Henry fawns all over her like the simpleton he is. Still the man comes when called and never complains that his errands are uninspiring. He seems to live simply to serve and run my kingdom, and mine it will be, once I claim Jenna; surely nobody could any longer refute my claim. She claims to be not of noble blood, and that she has no recollection of her beginnings, but any fool can see by the way she carries herself that she is meant for great things.

Anthony clears his throat behind me, as though I had not detected his presence. I continue to watch, as Jenna looks down at herself and has a clear struggle to contain a flair of temper. Henry has gestured in the direction of her suite, which I always keep ready for her. She leaves the entryway, sweeping up the stairs for all the world like she is already lady of the house.

I turn then and take in the sight of Anthony, cocking a brow at his newly-healed nose, and possibly jawbone, clearly she'd done a number on him before conceding to visit. This to me is a double-edged sword, I desperately want to make Jenna mine. However, I love that she refuses to heel like all the other simpering idiots that try to catch my attention daily. Not that I need her support, my patron is very powerful and together we can accomplish much.

There is a general feeling between us, that if I were to subvert Jenna's will by making her my own, then perhaps the way might be easier. "It appears that you might have upset the princess..." I leave that open-ended and simply wait for a response.

Anthony snorts, "You could say that! I did as you suggested and made a bit of a move, tried to provoke her, and she just bloody snapped. Smacked me in the jaw with an ashtray, I think it was, and broke my nose. She almost lost control but pulled it back, at the last minute, and threw me clean across the room. I didn't realize she was so strong, you might have warned me!"

I look him over without responding and start to walk away. Jenna is clearly better-controlled than I had thought, and I need time to ponder. "Go and change," I call back over my shoulder "Have Henry incinerate those clothes, I don't need any issues this week!"

5

Waiting

Jenna

I truly hate the thought of being stuck here for even just this night, let alone the whole week. I wonder if this is just another ploy at getting me to subjugate myself to him, or if Marcus actually has anything to say that I might be interested in hearing. The answer, of course, is not usually, so I have little hope of today being different. I suppose I should change then, since I am covered in Anthony's blood. My clothes and jacket will need burning, and I feel the rage start to slowly bubble inside me. I am going to need to get a grip on myself, before I start casually removing heads, for little to no reason, at all.

A quiet knock at the door pulls me from my reverie, and

I am happy to see Henry with a stack of practical-looking clothes. I have no doubt that the wardrobe will still be stuffed with flouncy ball gowns and satin cocktail dresses, as usual. The fact that Henry has taken the time to arrange this for me, I find quite touching and I offer him a slightly wan smile. Our relationship has always been a good one, and honestly, Henry is the closest I have to a father figure. I like the fact that he knows me and my preferences; he quietly gives me information so that I might control my temper in Marcus' presence. He has previously brought favoured books for me to read when I was here, and if I felt particularly low, he played the piano forte for me. I love Henry's playing, he seems to have natural talent and flare for music.

This place has a strange resonance for me. It feels comforting and almost like a true home should, but this is Marcus' little kingdom and I cannot stand to be in his presence, for any length of time. He stalks around the place like the lord of the manor but truth is; his position here was handed to him by the Lady Camilla. He had basically brownnosed enough, since his Turning, that she had placed him here as her regent when she had tired of him.

Marcus seems to conveniently forget that I had been present for his Turning. I had seen him beg for mercy from the predatory vampires who had singled him out for their evening games. I had watched, as I was required to do in those days, as they played with him, torturing his mind with offers of freedom in return for supplication, and then torturing his body for his quick agreement to do so. It truly was a shock to all when he rose on the third night. He'd been left for dead and put out for the scavengers. They say he must have buried himself in the forest to have survived the first three days unprotected.

When he returned to the castle, he was hailed a survivor and given a place in court. Initially, Marcus was a reasonable individual. He was relieved to have survived the night and be given a place with us, although he hadn't bargained for any such thing at any point during his begging. He tried to build relationships with those of us in residence at the time. Those first few decades passed with very little incident.

Then he seemed to change, Lady Camilla returned from a trip, without her consort, and anyone that asked after him was told, in no uncertain terms, not to ask again.

Mystery also seemed to surround the trip that Camilla taken, both its location and purpose were closely guarded, even from the inner court. I watched with interest as it became more than obvious that Marcus had been taken as Juan's replacement in Camilla's bed.

I watched Marcus change from the well-liked, personable vampire he had been initially, into the preening, pompous peacock that he is today. He began barking orders at anyone and everyone, while Camilla smiled indulgently. She made it obvious with her complete indifference that no argument or complaint would be brooked.

The atmosphere at the nest had begun to change, too.

Our main nest had ever, in my memory, been a place of welcome for those that followed the rules, those that hid the secret and did not endanger our kind, and that began to slowly change. The doors were metaphorically closed, for the first time in centuries. It was rumoured that Camilla and Marcus would experiment with their prey before dispatching them, sometimes screams were heard from below, in the newly forbidden dungeons.

Vampires started leaving, those that had been at court would suddenly disappear and were replaced with others. I heard rumours that Camilla and Marcus had started experimenting on vampires and other supernaturals and that some of those from court who had left, had not been heard from again.

That was when Henry had entered my life, he had made an impression upon Camilla and she had then allowed him to keep her house for her, having been a butler in his former life. Her respect for him seemed almost reverent, and he had a presence that filled me with hope. He almost seemed to be holding the seeping Darkness at bay, and I for one was grateful for his arrival.

I had felt like I was drowning, like I was being tainted from the inside out. At that time, I was still very much in awe of Camilla and did not have the strength of mind to oppose her change of direction. I was still grateful for her acceptance, and I did not wish to incite her anger by disagreeing. After all, I remembered nothing of life outside the castle then, I just felt that her actions were somehow wrong.

Henry talked with me when his duties would allow, sometimes I would find him in the library reading dusty tomes of our histories. They had never interested me, and indeed, whenever I did catch sight of the pages within, they seemed almost as though written in code. I once asked Henry how he could read such writings, and he had replied, "Truth and knowledge will reveal itself, only when the questioner is properly prepared." Which at the time had made no sense to me. Looking back now, I think he was just telling me that if I learned its language, then I would understand its words, if not its teachings. Something like that anyway.

One day, Henry suggested that it might be wise for me to leave Germany. I had been thinking the same way myself, but having no memories of the world outside, I did not have the courage to go. I felt that to leave would be to run away from whatever was manifesting itself here, but to run blindly into the unknown was paralysingly terrifying to me.

I was Vampire, yes, but I was an old vampire with absolutely no memories of my life before. Logically, there must be some reason for that, and nothing I could think of lead to good things being on the other side of the castle wall.

Henry told me of his good friend, Larisa, who, he assured me, would be only too happy help me find my way and learn to live again. Fortunately, the day that I chose to request permission to leave Camilla's court, some kind of emergency erupted during our meeting, and she waved me away impatiently to deal with it.

Sometimes, I wonder how much more I have to thank Henry for. He certainly looked after me then and has continued to mediate through my increasingly strained and painful working relationship with Marcus ever since.

6

Refusal

Jenna

One day turned into a week, and that week quickly turned into a month. Simply being present in the chateau left me obliged to attend the nightly parties, balls, and other such nonsense that made up the majority of life here. Had I been anyone else, then it may well have been enjoyable. As it was, I found myself proverbially pulling my hair out with frustration.

Marcus keeps putting off the meeting for which I have been summoned, saying something has come up, or just give me a few hours. Let me deal with everything else first, seems to be the message, and yet, I am not allowed to leave because it is of vital importance that we speak.

I spend my days in the library reading, sometimes I look over our history books and other times I look to 'popular' fiction tales of vampires and the supernatural. Most I find to be almost laughable in their depiction of us, and some paint a picture so close to our reality, I wonder if the writers had been a supernatural creature themselves or at the very least had known one intimately.

During the evenings and nights, I escape to the woods when I can, but most often there is some nonsense to be attended. Apart from Henry, I have no one here with whom I can talk, or even spend time, without battling my rage, and unfortunately he has his duties to attend to. He does, however, come to me whenever he can and suggests books I have not noticed before. Had I actually chosen to spend my time this way, it would have been enjoyable to learn our histories in more depth, but my mind is distracted.

I keep thinking of the boy in the club, who had tried to save me. He'd shown such courage in even talking to me, since I always wear a repellent glamour. Usually humans avoid me, without even realizing they are doing so. The only time I break the glamour, is to move in on my mark. I am having trouble understanding how I was that distracted as to let someone through. Although, I suppose if he were some kind of supernatural, then he may simply be able to see through it. I don't think this can be the case though or surely he would also have known me for what I am.

As time continues to march forward, I grow

increasingly irate with the whole charade. Marcus clearly has some reason for making me wait, which I cannot fathom. Even the thought of him somehow getting what he wants is as infuriating as being made to wait.

Eventually after almost seven weeks of this tedium, I have had all I am going to take. As I stalk through the castle, it seems to me that the others are conspicuous in their absence. I am not to be deterred as I unceremoniously fling open the door to Marcus' study.

"Geneviève, Mon Tresor!"

"Marcus, I am NOT, never have been, Nor WILL I ever be your treasure! Now what in the Seven Shades do you want? You summoned me here almost seven weeks ago now, and it has been party after party and insufferable tedium. I want to know why I am here enduring this and you will not avoid answering again!"

"Mon Ange...."

"No! You are not French, damn it! You may have set yourself up as lord high and mighty in a restored French chateau, but that doesn't make you French. Now stop stalling and tell me what you bloody want!"

Marcus stands watching me wrestle with my anger, and smirks that self-satisfied smirk that he always seems to wear when he's getting what he wants. I suddenly realize, what he wants is my anger. He wants me to throw a hissy fit and lose my temper. That's probably what all the bloody parties were for, to wear down my patience and push my self-control to its limit. That supercilious, pompous bastard! The realization that he's played me for a fool is almost too much to contain, and my eyes burn crimson before I can pull it back in. His smirk turns into a full grin and he's on me before I can move.

"That's it, Jenna, let the monster out to play..." He's breathing in my ear and pinning me to the wall. I'd forgotten how strong he is. I need to gain control of myself...

"Let her out, my beauty, I've missed you and I need my queen by my side!" Actually, my 'monster' hates him, too. Although it rankles, she knows the best way to get out of this is not to fight, but to hide. I feel her pulling back, allowing me to regain my composure again.

Looking up, I catch his red eyes with my violet ones, and I can see the disappointment flash across his face before he shuts it down.

"Marcus," I say, sounding as calm as the moat waters outside. "We have been through this before. You have tagged my monster as being someone she simply is not. You assume that we will fall into line with your wishes and demands, simply because your monster wants it to be so. We are not willing to be your queen––ever! No amount of baiting and having people call me 'princess' will EVER change that fact. I despise your chosen lifestyle and I want nothing to do with it. Now, please, let me go, so that I may leave for home and we might continue pretending to be friends." I stop speaking and do not move. I simply gaze at him in as calm and nonthreatening way as possible, given the fact that he still has me pinned to the wall and is pressed against me in a decidedly sexual manner. This could go either way, really. He could lock me up with silver and force me to submit, should he want to, but I kind of think one of the reasons he wants me so much is simply because I keep saying no.

Marcus has convinced himself, over the years, that one day my monster will take full control of me. That I'll give up fighting the Darkness and let it consume me, at which point I'll come crawling back, begging for him to make me his whore and allow him to parade me around like a fucking doll. If he has to force it, then of course, he still wins, but if I'm silver poisoned; it will burn him too whenever he touches or bites me. Not really the ideal situation and plenty painful for me.

Running his nose down the side of my face, I force myself to remain calm, even though I suspect he might bite me. I have always managed to avoid being marked until now. He'll have a direct tap into my emotions if he tastes my blood. He lingers and I know that if I flinch, even slightly, he'll do it; he wants the excuse that his monster reacted to my fear. But I don't move and he lets go of me, taking one last deep inhale of my neck before moving back.

"My apologies, Chere, you are so intoxicating I wish to make you mine. I have no wish to displease you. Of course, you may go if you wish. You are my guest, not my prisoner, but I do sincerely hope you will visit again soon. Do not leave it so long next time..."

He flicks his hand casually towards the door as he turns away. I am out of it and in my room drawing deep, unnecessary, but calming, breaths before it has closed behind me.

I have no desire to wait for Henry to find me a carriage back to the village, so I run instead. It's quicker anyway and I really don't want to be in the chateau a second longer. I feel a burning need to get home and pick up where I left off. It definitely has nothing to do with the crystal blue eyes I see every time I close my own, or the smell of home and safety that I am craving like my life depends on it.

———————

Jenna

As the train finally pulls into the station, I breathe a rather belated sigh of relief at being home. Not that I miss the hustle and bustle of city life exactly, but this is where I'd chosen to settle for a while, and returning felt like finally stepping out from under Marcus' shadow. Not forgetting, of course, there's a lot more Darkness to be found in cities than in little villages. People don't notice so easily, when the odd person disappears on a night out. I close down my senses, as I have no wish to hunt this night, I just want to lie in my own bed.

Leaving the town behind, I work my way out to the surrounding hills where I keep a secluded cottage. It's much more homey and comfortable than my apartment in town, but since it is a fair distance, I don't come here all the time. I am feeling overstimulated, after my long visit to the nest. I just want some time in my own space before I step back into the routine. My cottage looks like any other little, derelict cottage, lost in the woods. From the outside, it ticks all the boxes: quaint, ramshackle, and abandoned. But as with the chateau, it's all glamour––oh, it's definitely ramshackle and quaint, but it's very secure.

I've owned this house for a long time, almost since I fled the nest, actually. Behind its worn, wooden front door is reinforced steel that should withstand the most determined intruder, supernatural or otherwise. In fact, all of the external walls have been reinforced with steel rods, and I have a bunker underground where I keep my most important and treasured belongings. I have artefacts from so far back I have no memory of obtaining them, or what they might be for. I just know they are important and must be protected––like Luc. What? Where did that come from?

I can feel my monster pricking her attention with interest, she seems to like Luc, too, and I'm not sure that's a good mix. He was so clearly Light on the night we met, that my logical mind rebels against the idea of interfering in his life. Equally, I just know I have to see those eyes again. Suddenly, I have no interest in the cottage and am changing into a new outfit, whilst refusing to analyse why it matters what I'm wearing.

7

Yearning

Luc

As I came out of the bathroom, I saw her standing there. As still as though she were a statue. Eyes closed like she was waiting for the room to stop spinning. I don't even know what caught my eye, but once I'd seen her, I couldn't stop staring. She was totally out of my league, in fact so far out of my league I'd probably need to fly international to get there.

What can I say; she was tall, dark, and gorgeous. Totally different from the kind of girl I'd speak to normally. However, I just knew I had to, and somehow, I knew she wouldn't look at me like I'd gotten stuck to the bottom of her stiletto boots. All the same, instinct made me steel myself against rejection or ridicule, but then she opened her eyes and looked straight into mine.

The room around me might as well have folded up and dropped into oblivion for all I could see it. I was totally drawn into her sparkling violet eyes, and I don't think I could have pulled away if I had wanted to.

Then she shot me down in flames. "Keep moving, Boy Scout, you are not my type!"

I just stood there like a moron, making a really good impression and not knowing what to say, other than... "Why?"

She just laughed and I don't blame her. She looked me up and down like she was surveying the menu and told me to get away from her. For some reason the way she said, "Immediately," struck a chord of fear through my heart, and I turned away, but my moron side turned me back.

"I'm Luc, by the way. Hope to see you around."

She looked at me as though I'd committed some kind of heinous crime and announced, "I know, but I'm leaving now. I've found my date."

With that she stalked away from me and up to Robbie the Rat. He was well known for his 'Hump 'Em and Dump 'Em' philosophy, and I couldn't bear the thought of this girl being one of his many conquests. As I watched, she walked right up to him and cut into his conversation with a girl I knew from my street. She turned him to look into her eyes, and he immediately followed her out of the club like a kitten being led to its food bowl.

"LUKE! We're going back to Mike's, you coming?"

It was my mates, apparently we were leaving for Mike's house. He lives with his parents, but they have money so why wouldn't he. They're away this weekend, so the plan was to occupy the pool house and entertain whatever girls we could find. Looks like I'd be playing gooseberry again.

'Yeah, mate, hold up!' It's better than staying here; at least I can watch TV and drown my sorrows.

So we're wobbling down the road, as you do, and I see my gorgeous vision in ankle boots, being pulled into an alley up ahead.

This is it, I think, my chance to shine and I speed up.

I wake with a start and realize I have been dreaming about the girl from the club again. I always have the weirdest mix of feelings afterwards, it's like instinctive terror and infatuation all at once. Maybe I'm terrified of not seeing her again?

Seven weeks it's been since that night. I still see her in my dreams every night, and every time I turned around, I expect to see her standing there watching me. The guys had realized I was looking for someone after the first couple of weeks. Now, not an evening goes past, they don't grab my arm and drag me up to some dark-haired beauty, announcing they've found my Cinderella. If only I actually had a glass slipper; that at least would be some physical thing to prove I wasn't as bat-shit crazy as they all think I am. I just hope they're not right and I'm actually just lost in a psychotic delusion.

My mother has taken to staring at me like I've grown an extra limb, or indeed like she's expecting me to, at any moment. She keeps touching my head and muttering to herself about taking my time, like she's waiting for something. You know, I do kind of feel like I'm waiting, but quite what for, I really couldn't say. She keeps going on about Celtic roots, and the time being now. Apart from the weird spelling of my name, she really hasn't mentioned us having Celtic roots before, so I'm not really sure what that's about. Unless she's reading too many fantasy novels, that might explain it I suppose. Apparently the world needs protecting and the time is now to prepare. Yesterday, I had found her in the attic, rooting about looking some for old book she wants to look at.

Anyway, I've got a late shift coming up, so I need to hurry myself along a bit; at least it's an extra opportunity to watch out for...her. God, I am completely obsessed and I don't even know her name!

8

Crossing Paths

Jenna

As I stroll through quaint, narrow streets, I find myself in the unusual position of not blocking my talent, but equally not really tuning into anyone either. I have no doubt that for the area I am currently walking, there will be plenty of Darkness to be found, but it isn't reaching out for me. I catch the odd glimpse and no more, no focus and no pull. I look at the faces of the people around me, I breathe deeply in and out, searching for that comforting homey scent from the first time. Nothing.

Can I have delusions? Maybe I imagined Luc out of some subconscious need for more, but how could I? Why would my mind create this confusion without reason? Surely, there must be some purpose.

The memory is so clear and vivid that it must have been real, or was it somebody else's memory that imprinted itself on me? No! I am absolutely talking myself in circles. He is real. I will find him because it seems to be imperative to my existence, and I can think of nothing else.

I hear sirens as the fire engine passes the end of the street, and I feel a vague pull but continue along my way, searching the crowd for the face I see in my mind.

––––––––

Luc

The sirens are screaming as we race through the town; someone needs our help and we rush to their aid. The building looks like an office of some kind, and we arrive as the windows blow out on the top floor. The report states that the alarm was triggered manually from there, which means we're going in, not just to fight the fire, but to search.

The air is thick with smoke before we reach the office suite at the top of the building. I honestly don't hold out much hope, but in our line of work, every life is precious and worth fighting for, so we search. Amazingly, we find the office owner not far from the doorway, unconscious on the floor. Security lists no one else unaccounted for in the building, and so we turn to leave, but some kind of movement catches my eye across the office.

I turn to look. I am absolutely certain that I have seen someone by the window. Every life is indeed precious, and without thinking, I go towards the movement, assured there is someone there. I really should have known better, and made my way around the outside of the room, but I instead I cross the centre. As I call back for aid, the floor collapses beneath my feet. I can hear the lads calling, and I know they will circle below to try and catch me, but my grip is slipping. I know there is nothing I can do to save myself.

The floor below is already engulfed in flames and I know that when I fall on to it, I will crash through to the floor below surrounded in fire. I try, of course, reaching and trying to stretch my flailing feet to find some secure foothold, but I know it's coming. I just wonder if the fall will kill me or if I'll burn. I really don't want to go either way, but I suppose the fall might at least be quick.

As my hand slips, and I start to fall, 'her' face flashes into my mind. Irrationally, I wish I could have at least known her name.

Suddenly a pale, slender hand is gripping mine and I seem to be falling upwards. I am moving really fast and my head is spinning. When the world stops moving, I find myself sitting on the roof of the next building and staring dazedly into a pair of glittering emerald eyes. She is staring at me like she's trying to look directly into my brain cavity.

"Will you live?" she enquires, almost as though she cares.

"Yes, I believe so, you saved my life?"

"Obviously."

"Thank you! What were you doing in the building?"

"Saving your life," she replies, raising an eyebrow like I might be simple.

"Of course, how stupid of me. Who are you? How did you pull me from the ledge?"

"My name is Ana. Boy, do you know who you are?"

"Well, yeah, since I've been me my whole life," I reply sarcastically, which is slightly ruined as I doubled over coughing.

"That's all well and good, but do you know who you TRULY are? Who you are destined to be...I am going to assume from that sardonic frown that the answer is no. Speak to your mother, boy, read the book, and then we can talk. But know this, I am watching, the stakes are high and the time is very nearly here. You are required for the final act; please take care of your mortal lifetime more effectively. I cannot always be here to save your arse!" With that she is gone, and as I slump over coughing again, I realize I have no idea how we have gotten here.

———

Ana

After leaving the boy behind, I sit watching from a nearby building. My left arm is burning from the fire and it hurts like holy hell. I shall have to feed this night or feel this wretched pain through the day. I watch as the firemen bring the blaze under control, and I see the boy as he emerges, still looking confused from the adjacent building. A cry goes up as he is spotted, and he is swooped upon by paramedics and firefighters alike, wanting, I imagine, to know how he got there. I wonder in passing what he'll say. My evening, however, is not yet done, it is well past time to set the pieces moving, and now I have to find dinner, too.

Moving across the rooftops, I decide to intercept Jenna. She has toiled so long on her own, and I have watched from the sidelines, never interfering. She has struggled to find meaning amongst the chaos and the Darkness, and I truly feel quite proud that she has managed so well. She has clung rigidly to her sense of right and wrong and tried, desperately at times, to create some good from a path that would be seen by most as pure evil. Depravity personified, with no hope of redemption, and yet she has rarely lost faith that there is a purpose to be found. If I were capable of such, I could almost say, I envied her for her strength and tenacity.

Jenna is prophesised and I have appointed myself the task of 'project management,' you could say. In the larger game, there are many players and many possible outcomes. I fully intend to win this round and Jenna is my ultimate weapon, she just doesn't know it yet!

Jenna

I smell fire, and remembering the fire engine passing, follow the sounds of chaos. All kinds of morbid individuals gather to watch tragedy unfold, and I suspect that I may find a suitable target amongst them. Rounding the corner, into what I assume is a business district, I walk smack into utter bedlam. There is indeed a crowd forming, and the police are trying to hold the idiots back and keep them from getting in the way. There are at least three fire crews in attendance, and flames are billowing from broken windowpanes on several upper floors.

My eyes are drawn to the next building, however, as a dirty and slightly unsteady figure emerges. The person is surrounded quickly by firefighters and paramedics. Idly, I wonder why they seem so confused. I only realize as they load him into an ambulance that I have been subconsciously drifting closer. Suddenly the crowd parts to close the ambulance doors, and the injured figure wearing an oxygen mask looks up, meeting my eyes. I feel a moment of panic; what on earth has happened? The panic is quickly followed by guilt at having not been here to stop this from happening in the first place. I listen in and I hear something about a wrenched shoulder and smoke inhalation, triggering psychosis. That doesn't sound good, or likely, when compared to the man I met in the club that night. He seemed so sensible, why would he run into a burning building with an injured arm? I feel really stupid as I notice he's wearing a fire fighter's uniform.

Everything starts to make a lot more sense, and again, I take in the structured chaos going on around me. I hear a startled intake of breath, which quickly turns into a hacking cough, and turn back to the ambulance in time to meet his bright blue eyes once more, as they close the doors. He looks exactly as I remember him, a bit grubbier obviously. If it were possible for my breath to catch, I really do think it would have. He's real and I am relieved, excited, and terrified at the same time.

The ambulance starts to move out. As I make to follow, I have the strangest sensation of being watched, but I can't exactly work out from where or by whom. I look around at the chaos and scan the surrounding buildings to try and pinpoint the sensation, but then it is gone. So I take to the rooftops to follow my ambulance.

Luc

She was there! I saw her, I'm sure I did. The ambulance crew keep trying to settle me down though, apparently I am delusional due to lack of oxygen. They are telling me it is not possible to fall upwards and land on the building next door, as if I didn't already know that. But that's really what happened, isn't it? How else do they think I got there? I clearly cannot fly with this arm pulled like it is.

That thought stops me, and I realize that maybe I am crazy. Of course, I can't bloody fly, injured arm or no injured arm. It is simply not possible.

Maybe I imagined 'her,' too then, maybe this whole

time I have been kidding myself. My mates were right; I have lost the plot. With that last thought I slip into unconsciousness.

————

Ana

As I turned to leave, I spot Jenna in the crowd. She catches his eye as they closed him into the ambulance, and I smile to myself. Perhaps I'll catch up with Jenna later. I am certain she'll be ambulance chasing in a moment. As I watch her scan the rooftops and crowd, I wonder if she can sense me yet. As she starts out after the ambulance, I decide that the answer is not yet.

9

Found

Jenna

I hate hospitals. My sense of smell is really on point and I can literally smell everything. It's bad enough to get a detailed ingredients list as you walk past a restaurant but when you are near a hospital...well, there are obviously all manner of bodily fluids, sickness, infection, despair, loneliness, and death. Hospitals are truly depressing places. I enter through a staff door and cloak myself in a glamour to appear as a doctor but attract no attention.

Glamour is a weird thing; it's like playing dress-up or hide-and-seek but completely inside your own head. I have been able to cast glamour with ease for as long as I can remember clearly, but I only realized recently that this is considered very unusual amongst my kind. Usually, a fully-fledged witch is needed for an effective glamour, but I seem to have an innate ability for it. This and my additional tele-sentient ability mark me as a freak within my own society, let alone other societies. I vaguely wonder what that might indicate from my past, or indeed, what it may mean for my future, but I push that thought aside.

Right now, I need to find Luc. I need to assure myself that he is fine. I move through the hospital with minimum fuss and establish that he has already been through triage and is awaiting a doctor to evaluate his condition. As he is left alone, I slip inside the cubicle still fully cloaked in glamour. I expect that he will call me doctor and answer my questions, whilst I look over his injuries. Instead, as I step inside, his eyes latch onto mine and his first words, "Are you real?" shock me, and I wonder if he hit his head as well this evening.

"I am," I reply calmly, as I take his arm to examine the shoulder.

Luc looks excited now and pulls at his oxygen mask. "It's me, Luc! Don't you remember me from the club the other week?" I freeze as I realize the implications of that question.

"You recognise me?" I ask quietly

"How could I not? I see your face in my dreams..." He instantly starts to blush, which looks really odd, considering his dirt-smudged cheeks, but it endears him to me all over again.

"Please?" he implores me. "I almost died tonight, without even knowing your name. Please, tell me your name?" He has captured my hand in his and doesn't seem to have noticed that I'm really quite chilly.

He stares hopefully into my eyes and I hear myself answer softly, "Of course, I remember, my name is Jenna, short for Genevieve."

"Jenna, I am so pleased to meet you, finally. I'm Luc, short for Lugus."

I can't move, like at all. He's still holding my hand, and I'm just standing by his bedside, completely stunned that he can see through my glamour. He seems to want to know me, as much as I feel, I need to know him.

Suddenly a real doctor steps into the cubicle and looks shocked at finding a 'colleague' in a fairly unprofessional situation with a patient. Quickly I disengage, and incline my head in his direction, trying to look sheepish. "Doctor, I'll excuse myself now and leave Luc to your slightly more objective assessment, if that's okay?" I don't wait for an answer; just slip away quickly before he realizes he doesn't know me.

Deciding that the roof might be a good place to wait and attempt to straighten my tangled thoughts, I head up the central stairwell. There I come face-to-face with a being so beautiful, I could quite possibly find her very tempting if I'd met her before Luc. She smiles at me from her position, leaning against the roof door. "My dear Jenna, I am honoured to finally make your acquaintance. My name is Ana."

Ana really is quite the vision: she has almond-shaped, sparkling emerald eyes, and a beautiful mane of deep red hair. I remember reading that strong magical ability is often symbolised with green eyes and red hair. I take an involuntary step back, realizing instantly that she was waiting here for me; this is no chance encounter.

Ana raises her hands slowly to the side of her body and stands up straight, smiling. I give her a quick scan to assess her strength and threat but am startled to realize I am getting nothing from her. I take another half-step back in preparation to run, if I have to. "You were watching me earlier," I accuse, realizing the truth.

"I was yes, very astute. I have, in fact, been watching over you for a very long time. Please do not be alarmed, Jenna, I offer you no threat. I have simply come to make myself known to you."

"If you have been watching me for so long, undetected, why now would you choose to reveal yourself?"

"Because, dearest, the time is coming and you must be ready for the storm or be drowned in the deluge!"

"That makes literally no sense, you realize?"

"Nor should it, for now you should follow your heart wherever it leads. Often its instructions seem illogical, but they absolutely must be followed. Ignore the heart to your own eventual destruction, dearest. Now remove your glamour and return to your boy. They will admit him for observations, but I suspect you'll still be able to manage a visit."

With that Ana was simply gone. I didn't think she had moved at speed; I am sure I would still have followed a movement however fast. She really did seem to have simply vanished and it startled me. The whole encounter had taken no more than two minutes I was certain. Sure enough, when I returned to Luc's cubicle, it was to hear the doctor reassuring him that they were just being careful but were admitting him overnight for observation.

He looked up into my eyes as I entered, and there it was again, that floor tilt thing. He reached out to take my hand and the floor levelled out again. I could no longer hear the doctor's words until there was a pointed throat clearing to my left. We both looked to the doctor, who was trying not to smile. Luc looked slightly abashed and apologised, while I released his hand and stepped back. The next few minutes were taken up by admission arrangements and moving Luc to the ward, but then we were alone.

For the very first time, in what feels like forever, I am really nervous. "So, you protect people from fire?" I start awkwardly

"Well, no, but kind of...I suppose. That makes it sound quite grandiose, and it's really not that exciting, well not, usually." Luc seems to be teasing not just me, but himself, and it appears to come so naturally I can't help but smile.

I sat with Luc through the night, watching over him while he slept and talking with him when he awoke.

I made sure he drank plenty of water to ease his parched throat. He seemed marginally surprised every time the nurse came in and just didn't seem to see me, but he didn't mention it so neither did I.

I felt a great need to stay close and make sure no further harm came to him. So I did exactly that, following my hearts instructions, even though it made no sense to me whatsoever. We talked about all manner of random and nonconsequential things, such as the weather last weekend, and whether or not Cadbury's Crème Eggs are actually reducing in size year on year.

We touched upon Luc's wish to protect people, which had led to his career decision and very vaguely that I felt an affinity with such logic. He told me that he had feared for his sanity after we met, and of his search for me since that night. Apparently his friends have been unkind about his obsession, and I clench my fists so as not to highlight my anger.

Through it all, I still can't really work out why I am here, or why I need to connect with this man so badly. He isn't triggering my need to feed, I just want to know him, I think, and that makes no sense to me. As daylight starts to dawn, I realize I am going to have to leave or face some awkward questions. I am also fairly certain that he would sleep more if I weren't here, so I make noises about getting to bed for a few hours. He looks upset, but I know he needs to sleep. I stand slowly to make a show of leaving, and Luc reaches for my hand, and I let him grasp it. "Will I see you again, Jenna? Or will this just seem like a dream, too?"

I pause as I try to decide whether he has actually realized this is a real possibility if I wish, or whether that's his way of asking me to come back. I decide to go with innocence as a response. "I'll come back around lunchtime, if you like. Maybe they'll let you out, and I can help you get home safely, since you're clearly incapable right now."

He gives me a self-satisfied, lopsided smile and settles back into his pillows, sleeping almost instantly. I melted into the shadows as I leave the building. I'll need to change before returning, since I am supposed to be going home to sleep. I don't actually sleep so I have plenty of time to kill it would seem.

10

Threats

"Marcus!" she bellows, stepping from the shadows and making him jump.

"Lady Danu! How did you get in here?"

"Really? That's your greeting? A more suspicious being might think you were struggling with a guilty conscience..."

"Of course not! You just surprised me... Which is something I am unaccustomed to. I am of course happy to welcome you to Chateau de la Mothe-Chandeniers!"

"Are you really, Marcus? Well now, that is a surprise." Stalking forward into his space, Ana asserted her dominance, placing a hand to her chin, making a show of looking thoughtful. "You see, the thing is, I know you laid hands on Jenna, and THAT makes me very unhappy! Tell me, why would you do such a thing?" Ana demanded, with her forefinger and deadly sharp nail pressed precariously close to Marcus' heart.

"She is mine!" Ana grabs Marcus and pins him to the floor

"NO! SHE! IS! NOT! If you ever mark her against her will, Marcus, I will rip your pretty, petty, little head from your shoulders! Am I making myself in anyway unclear?"

"No, My Lady, I understand. Please forgive me...? Allow us to offer the hospitality accorded to your birthright, Lady Danu!" Marcus stammered clearly ruffled and hoping to retain his head. Ana allowed him to stand, and looked him over slowly, before turning her back and moving slowly to the window, demonstrating her complete disregard for him.

Ana

I could totally see why Jenna hated this place so much. Its residents were full of their own self-importance, and the chateau itself, although very beautiful, felt like a prison with its moat and single bridge. Very defensible, yes, but surely it was depressing to have to live in such a way. I suppose, being highly flammable, Marcus might be more than a little paranoid about fire. In that sense, the moat offered a chance of survival, should someone attack castle and try to burn it and its inhabitants. I wondered idly whether Marcus had ever thought to have an escape tunnel built into the bottom of the moat, for such an event. Vampires, having no need to breathe, would surely benefit from such a tunnel and it could go on indefinitely.

I hear Marcus rise behind me and turn to look at him, eyebrows raised, awaiting his next attempt to pacify my anger.

"Lady Danu, I once again offer you my sincere apologies for my insubordination and persistent pursuit of Jenna. I hadn't truly realized that she was untouchable by way of edict, Madam."

"You snivelling little snot, Marcus. It should matter not whether she is untouchable or not. If someone says no to your advances, then the answer is bloody NO. You do not force the issue or make it the punishment for misdemeanours. I know you colour yourself as king in this little kingdom, but never forget, you are the lowest of the low as far as I am concerned. You really do not want my estimation of you to drop any lower. The time for change is coming, and if you are not careful, you will be swept away with the tide and replaced. I, for one, will not mourn your passing, Marcus. Maybe you should bear that in mind."

"Of course, Lady, I shall take note of your advice and review my actions accordingly. Might I summon Henry, to serve you some lunch, or perhaps you will honour us with an extended visit?"

"Yes, thank you, I will see Henry and perhaps eat here. But I will not accept your invitation to visit on this occasion; I am very busy, as I am certain you must be, too. I shall be on my way shortly, I have business in your library first however."

"As you wish My Lady. Mi casa, es su casa as always"

"Yes, Marcus, your house is indeed my house, and always will be. Ah, Henry dear, just in time. Would you kindly escort me to the library and then perhaps have cook make me some lunch?" Bowing, Henry offers me his arm and we walk away from Marcus. I hear him exhale a sigh of relief. It would seem I had played my part well and put the fear of destruction into him. Not that I wouldn't carry out my threats, if I had to, but it really was more for show than anything else. I had no real concern that he would overstep his mark, or that Jenna couldn't put him in place, should she actually need to. Besides which, she would have her protector in place soon. The boy's change should trigger anytime now and then they would be an unmatchable team. So far so good.

Henry and I have known one another since his creation, in fact unbeknown to his 'master,' he is mine and his loyalty has never been questioned. Henry knows this building like nobody else, including all of its secrets both known to Marcus and unknown. "Henry dear, how have you been?"

"As well as ever, My Lady. I am ever in your service, as you know, and I find the Master and his habits to be tedious beyond all reason."

"I know, Henry, I appreciate your efforts as always and offer you my thanks. Did you find the item?"

"I did, Madam, the rumours are that it can be found 'Over the misty mountains old, through dungeons deep and caverns cold.' What that means though, Madam, I couldn't say."

"I see, well that is a riddle, indeed. Thank you for taking the time though, Henry. I can find my way from here. If Cook could put me together some fruit, I would be most grateful, and perhaps something to help this arm to hurry along."

With that, Henry bowed and left me to continue into the library proper, where I proceed to make a show of looking for something. I casually pick up a first edition copy of *The Hobbit,* as though completely at random, amongst other titles, some of which included witchcraft tomes and mythological texts, since that is what I would be expected to be looking for here. Not that I needed reminding, since I'd written most of the damned histories in the first place, but only Henry and I knew that. Whilst sifting the books in front of me, I was able to retrieve the small package from within the pages of Bilbo's adventures and slip it into my pocket to look at later.

After twenty minutes or so, I returned the books to the stacks and made a mental note to take the chateau from Marcus and restore this library, it was completely wasted on this nest. None of them were interested in the histories, fictitious or not, or in reading generally, it would seem. I thought idly that Jenna would probably enjoy this library, if it were in the home of anyone but Marcus. With that thought

I left, pretending to not know I was being watched. I headed back to the kitchen for my lunch, which I would eat, tainted or not, so that Marcus would know he was no match for me. He would not win in such a crude manner.

11

Fairy Tale Awakening

Luc

Waking in the hospital was a bit surreal, to be honest. I kind of thought the whole thing had been another dream, especially the bit where my fantasy woman actually seemed to like me and want to know me. Now I am sitting here in the hospital, waiting for a doctor to decree I can leave.

Apparently, my shoulder was wrenched quite badly, and with some questionable force, but will reset without help and is already markedly better than expected. The smoke inhalation I suffered was nothing above the ordinary for my chosen profession, so I am essentially good to go and just awaiting a green light. But sitting here waiting, remembering her face, I can't help but wonder if I also bumped my head. I mean that can't all have been real, can it? And as for the red-haired woman that saved me... No, must have bumped my head. So, I start wondering if I should mention my delusions to the doctor. Then in she walks. The raven-haired beauty from my imagination, she looks pale and ill at ease, but otherwise, exactly as I remember, with striking violet eyes and long wavy hair. She's holding a box of chocolates and I'm wishing she was visiting me, when over she strolls without a care in the world.

"Hey, how are you feeling today?" she asks, looking for all the world like she's nervous, whilst handing me the chocolates

"Err, like I woke up in a fairy tale. You're blind, right, and looking for the guy that was in this bed yesterday?"

Her lips twitch as she looks me over and her eyes soften when they meet mine. "I feel a bit like that too, Luc. I am not really sure why I'm here..."

She looks so lost in that moment of self-questioning, that I see myself reflected in her eyes. Suddenly, I am really scared that I may have found what I have been looking for my whole life. I feel as though I won't be able to breathe when she's not here; I won't be able to think for wondering where she is and whether she is safe.

I feel an overwhelming urge to protect her from the world and it absolutely takes my breath away. My internal monologue starts up with its admonitions, *'Don't be ridiculous, you have only just met, she cannot possibly be vital to your existence, you fool. She looks more than capable of taking care of herself, whoever said she needs or even wants a protector. You're not good enough!'*

I feel crushed in that instant and she frowns. "Stop it, Luc. Whatever you're telling yourself, it looks painful. Please don't…"

Before I can answer, Dr. Carter strolls over to introduce himself and offers Jenna his hand, which for some reason he frowns at. "Sorry," she apologises. "Bad circulation."

"Ah, now, Luc. You've been a very lucky boy. I've been over your X-rays and test results. I can see no reason to worry about lasting damage to your airways, and although the injury to your shoulder is considerable, other than resting it, there really isn't much we can do. How did you say it happened?"

"I fell through the floor and grabbed the edge as I went down."

"Well, yes, that makes sense, but to be honest, I would have expected you to be a much bigger man for the strain your shoulder was put under. Still, as I said, there doesn't look like there will be any lasting damage, but I'd like to see you back at the end of the week, just to double check, okay?"

"Sure thing, Doc. So, can I go? I kinda need a shower."

"Absolutely, I'll get the nurse to pop over with your discharge notes in a few minutes, and then you can be off."

As the doctor walks away, I glance up at Jenna, and without thinking; ask what she has planned for the rest of the day.

"Well, I thought you might need some help getting home safely, with that arm in a sling, and then well...I hadn't gotten that far, to be honest."

I offer her a slightly pained and crooked smile. "Help home sounds really good."

The crow that was listening and watching through the open window flew off as the pair readied themselves to leave together.

12

Encouraging Signs

Ana

I sat quietly reviewing what I had witnessed. The children seemed to be moving forward and trying to build a relationship, or friendship of sorts, without any encouragement, which was good. If we have to prompt it, then it won't be as binding, and the bond is all-important. The time was coming where we would all be tested and only the strongest would survive. Of course, it was not all about strength of muscles; it was also about strength of mind and sense of conviction. We would all be in very real danger if we had no true faith in ourselves. What was coming was, in a sense, a form of natural selection, and there were certainly many I would not miss when they failed, as I knew they would.

I withdrew from my pocket the package I had retrieved from the library in Marcus' nest. It was perhaps not the most sensible place to have hidden the amulet, but I always have had an ironic sense of humour. It amuses me to know how much Marcus would have loved to lay his hands on this little piece of Magick.

The pendant was as beautiful as I remembered, the goddess symbolism was obvious to those with open eyes. The depths and variance of colour in the rainbow topaz were simply mesmerizing, as they were meant to be. Made of sterling silver it was certainly eye-catching and, of course, lethal to most vampires. Jenna would suffer no ill effects from it though, since her specific physiology rendered her largely unaffected by most things. Not that I imagined she would know that yet. The resistance still needs to be built up over time, no matter how marvellous the latent talent maybe. Jenna's transition was really still in its early stages, but with the protector now in place, I could foresee a much quicker forward momentum. I was pleased to note the boy was strong too, even prior to his change, such very encouraging signs. I thought back to The Prophesy.

'Imbued with the power of the four, they will bring balance and unity to the community that needs them. They face all opposition with grace and valour for the good of all.'

The Morrigan

Yes, the signs were all very encouraging, and I felt that

the doorway was closer now than ever before, it almost felt within reach. My siblings and I had long known this time would come. Between us, we had ensured that the children grew strong and resilient as they would need to be. They are the key to all and our eventual salvation in an increasingly hostile world. Strong leadership is needed to survive the coming storm. I could only hope that I'd done my job adequately and that some of those important to me would survive.

Soon I would need to talk with my siblings and prepare.

13

Decisions

Jenna

Over the coming weeks, Luc and I grew closer, against my better judgement. We saw each other almost every night, and I always felt empty when we parted. I tried to vaguely give the impression that I worked, and as such, rarely met Luc during daylight hours. It doesn't hurt per se, but it's uncomfortable and makes me feel weak and unwell. We grew closer even as my sense of unease at my deception also increased.

I was in such a moral dilemma, even more than usual. I still needed to feed, but it now felt like I was living a lie. The murderers and rapists were the same Darkness they had always been, and I still craved their Darkness to nourish my own dark soul. However, I could see the Light in the world now too and...I don't know. My unease in general was growing stronger about everything, it seemed. I toyed, almost seriously, with the idea of closing up my home for a while and just leaving town, and stop interfering with the course of Luc's life, because that's what it felt like I was doing. I had absolute confidence that my home would remain secure in my absence, it had been previously. But would Luc be safe? Could I be certain that another of my kind, perhaps following my trail, wouldn't happen across him? Was it even right that I cared?

I sat in my favourite chair, watching the flames of the open fire, whilst I wrestled these thoughts. It seemed to me that if I cared for him, in any way, I should go. Equally, to do so might condemn him in some way I could not foresee. As I stared into the flames, willing an answer to present itself, I became aware of a knocking sound from the window. Turning, I looked into the eyes of a ridiculously large crow, who seemed for all the world like it had been watching me and now wanted to come in. Turning back to the flames, the knocking began again and proceeded to get louder until I rose, walking to the window and flinging it open, meaning to shoo the bird away.

Instead, it hopped through without the slightest delay, made itself comfy in the chair opposite mine, and promptly turned into a red-haired woman!

"Do shut the window, dearest, it is rather cold," Ana

chirped, with an amused look at my rather obvious shock.

I complied, of course, because what else would I do and returning to my seat looked her over.

"'I seem to have underestimated how much of a nuisance you might be to me," I said stiffly. "Nobody comes here but me, nobody knows where it is. I have always made sure it was secure."

"If you never intended to have company, why then place a second chair by the fire?"

"What, how, just...what?"

Ana laughed at my confusion and shook out her hair. "Dearest, don't worry about it. Your home is as safe as it ever was. If it makes you feel better, I would not enter without an invitation."

Raising my eyebrow, about to point out that she just had, again Ana laughed and waved away the notion that anything was wrong. I am now wondering if I am overly paranoid or if she has completely lost her marbles.

"Oh, I never had any marbles to lose, dearest, I don't see the point."

She's carrying on about the weather and my security being good for the coming storm, whatever that means. When it occurs to me; I never mentioned her marbles out loud.

She looks at me then and gives me a knowing smirk.

"Dearest, do you know who you are?" she asks, completely ignoring the fact that I just realized she's reading my thoughts. I can't overlook this. I am the only other being, known to me, that has any kind of telepathic power, and I am staring at her like she's sprouted a third leg.

Ana tilts her head and gives me a sidelong look. "I see we are going to have to discuss this, and I promise we will, but again I ask you, do you know who you are?"

"To be completely honest with you, right now I am more interested in knowing who or what you are."

"I, however, am more concerned with your current inner debate. It is rather important to me that you don't make any hasty decisions to leave your young man, until you at least have some real information to base your decision on." I go to ask how she knew my plan, and then shake my head and instead ask why it is so important to her.

"The storm is coming, I told you this."

"What does that even mean?" I bellow, startling the mind reader, which I am vaguely impressed about, in a detached kind of way. I start pacing the study. "You come in here. You've clearly been following me around. You talk in riddles and expect me to just accept it. Sit down and listen when I talk, well NO!" I almost shout and start tapping my forefinger impatiently upon the polished walnut desk that I never use but love anyway. "You clearly need something from me. You're not getting it until I know, what you are dragging me into, why, and what it involves, EXACTLY!"

Ana bows her head slightly in my direction. "Of course, but would you please sit down while we talk? You are making me slightly dizzy, and you are in very real danger of damaging your lovely desk." She makes this statement in a completely serious tone, but I just *know* that like me, there is no way she feels dizzy ever, let alone right now because I'm pacing. I also find it hard to believe she gives a damn about my desk. But I sit, feeling better for venting and making sure to continue frowning to make my point. Ana smiles at me indulgently, like she knows all this, and as she gets comfortable, I reflect that truthfully, she probably does.

"Ana, who are you?" I repeat.

"Dearest, I am the voice in your dreams that you turn to for advice in the face of your despair. I am your most ruthless protector, and I would do, and indeed have done terrible things, to keep you safe. I am the shadow that is always over your shoulder."

"That's all very interesting, of course, but doesn't really answer my question, does it?"

"Well, of course not, dear, where would be the excitement in that? I do however have a story to tell you, if you'll allow?" I wave my hand to signal she should proceed, since it is clearly the only way to get to the bottom of this weirdness. Settling back into her chair, she begins seriously.

"In the beginning there was only darkness and the cool calm depths of my being. I was vast, powerful, and calm but with the potential for tempest.

"I am the Lady of Lakes and Rivers. I have the infinite elemental strength of water to play with as I see fit.

"Slowly I became aware of another, of soft tickling caresses against my limits. Arren, the name came to me unbidden, but I knew it was important. My lover, my brother, another facet of myself. Together we would be stronger; together we belonged. So, I welcomed his attention and we danced together in my waves, making beautiful shapes in the foam.

"Our joy brought into being many sea creatures and aquatic plants, which transformed our lives into an ever increasing oasis of colour and life.

"Soon we discovered we were not alone. Along the edges of my consciousness, I became aware of another and her mate. Our siblings had joined, as we had, and their joy too had brought life into being. They parented many different species of land creatures, as well as trees and plant life.

"Delighted to find each other, our happiness was then complete. Each of us felt that the other three were the missing pieces of ourselves, and that we should remain always together so that we might be complete. None could imagine a more fulfilling life than that which we had made for ourselves. We felt peace."

"You're wanting me to believe you are some kind of elemental water being?"

"I am Danu, Goddess of Lakes and Rivers, I am The Universal Mother and Keeper of the Knowledge, Wisdom, and Prophesies."

"So you're all-powerful, and yet you have come for tea with me?"

"Not really, dearest, you didn't offer me any tea."

"Oh, erm, yes, of course. Sorry. Would you like some tea?"

"Yes, thank you, dear. That would be lovely."

How in the name of the Seven Shades of Hell did I end up making this woman tea? Why do I even have tea? I don't tolerate tea, I never have guests, and had not intended to... Why do I own tea?

"Because secretly, you knew I was coming, darling, and I prefer the pomegranate," chimes in Ana from the study, as I flick on the kettle I bought last week.

"So, back to your story. It all sounds very idealistic. What happened?"

Settling back with her tea, Ana looked into the flames as though watching her memories play out in the fireplace.

"Well, as you obviously realize, there is more to the story, or we wouldn't be having this conversation. What happened is that disagreements arose.

"Fire argued that I had more space than he and threatened to scorch the skies if I would not yield. I refused, obviously, the seas are home to vaster numbers of creatures than survive on land. I would not condemn them to death for the petty jealousies of my brother, and so there was war.

"Fire erupted from the earth, throwing ash into the skies and creating new land masses where magma touched my waters. Mountains thrust up from the earth, and some of my children were trapped in newly-formed inland seas, where they had to adapt or die.

"And I, well Arren and I, sought our revenge. I am ashamed to say that we sent rains to move across the earth, creating floods and killing many. Rivers formed where none had been before, and landmasses fell into the sea, buffeted by hurricane winds and thrashing waves.

"Many, many creatures died during the wars, both from the land and from the sea, and yet still we could not agree.

"One day it all changed, of all the children we four siblings had brought into being, none had been truly born. Our children, all the land and sea creatures, were not a physical representation of ourselves, like we witnessed the humans creating, but more a symbolic representation of our powers. We knew we were the creators, the holders of the magic, but we didn't really understand it.

"The next child, however, was different, she was made of our blood and our bodies. Created by our physical love one for the other.

"The night of that child's conception was more extreme than usual. My blood was drawn at some point and Arren licked the wound. He became cold and distant, although not for long. Almost immediately, he snapped out of it and the moment was all but forgotten.

"In the following days, however, it became clear to us that something unusual was happening to me, and we tried to understand what it was. Strangely, it was witnessing the birth of a dolphin that made it finally click into place, and with a huge sense of disbelief we tried to get used to this new situation.

"The child was born during the winter months, so it was some days before we realized that her skin was naturally cold. Not ice cold but like deep waters. We also had difficulty feeding the child, who seemed unable to tolerate fruits such as we preferred. She seemed instead to be fascinated by the small animals that frequented our home, and one day we witnessed her catch a passing rabbit and drink from its neck.

"The difference it made to her strength was obvious and her growth quickened when allowed to drink. We realized then that her diet was 'specialised' and that we would need to teach her restraint. Her strength seemed comparable to Arren's and my own, which we found understandable, and she seemed to have far deeper magical potential than even we could determine.

"As the child grew, Arren and I were also growing but in different directions. We would spend less and less time together as the world around us developed and moved forward, and so our interests and responsibilities also moved forward. We decided that the child should perhaps mix with the people of the world, rather than just the creatures, and so we set out to find her a human caregiver.

"This was not an easy task to accomplish, and initially, we thought it might prove impossible. Three were found drained of all blood before we thought to try and change one into a blood drinking creature. Two more did not survive our attempts to change them.

"Then we discovered Camilla, there was something in her manner, an almost regal quality that I felt certain would serve her well, and so I was proved correct. Not only did she survive the night, but she thrived in her new form, and with a little persuasion was made to forget that she was not, in fact, the first vampire. Instead she remembers caring for a child that did not survive. We felt the child's future would be more secure that way. So the Lady Camilla was allowed to flounce around, calling herself the Queen of the Damned as was her wont in those days, and of course she procreated. The Vampire race was increased exponentially by her hand. It became easier to conceal the child's existence and ensure her safety, which was obviously, even with all the distractions, of paramount importance to Arren and myself––even now in fact."

"So the child still lives?"

"Oh yes, Jenna. The child is still very much alive and still of paramount importance. We removed her from Camilla's care after a spell. It seemed to us that Camilla had grown jealous of the child's beauty and strength. It was almost as though she could remember, however indirectly, and grew to consider her a threat.

"We modified the memories of any that had known the child. They believe she died and they grieved for her loss."

"After a spell? How long exactly does a water goddess consider to be 'a spell'?" I enquired incredulously.

"A hundred? Two hundred years? I forget, darling."

"So, what happened to the child?" I asked, shaking my head

"We set her upon a new path. One that would help her grow," Ana replied vaguely

"Are there other children of this type?"

"There was one other, yes. A male child was born to Fire and Earth. He too was gifted, but he was mortal, and therefore lives only fleeting mortal lifetimes before returning to us again. We have followed the mortal descendants of this child for many centuries, and especially when he reincarnates; always as a male and always with piercing blue eyes. In every lifetime, he has displayed a need to save and protect others, although never before as strongly as this time..."

"And...you are telling me this big, complicated story because...?"

"You, my dearest Jenna, are the girl child. My child, whom I have protected for eons until the time was right to move forward."

I raised an eyebrow and sighed, "I assume you're now going to tell me who the boy child is, and that we have to hook up immediately to bring the four of you back together?"

"You are half-correct, sweet. The boy child is already known to you, and should you choose to 'hook up,' it will be your choice and for your own reasons. Any good to the rest of the world, or us, would be purely incidental."

"Go on then, it's bloody Marcus. Isn't it? And I have to leave Luc no matter my wishes."

"Oh goodness, no! He is in fact your own dear fireman, Lugus, my dear, and we have no wish for you to leave his side ever again."

I sit back in my chair staring. Ana continued to sit opposite, cool as a cucumber, sipping her tea as though she hadn't just tipped my world on to its arse. Having no memories prior to the nineteenth century, I really had no firm beliefs surrounding our origin as a species. Since my acceptance into Camilla's nest in Germany, I had always known her as our ruler, the first of our kind. Even though she herself claimed to know nothing of how she came to be. She had always been revered in my memory and respected as our queen, even after the rumoured experiments started, and I had never questioned it.

Now here sits Ana; in her very extremely obvious magicalness, telling me a completely different history than is written in our history books and expecting me to…to what? Accept that I am the true queen? The first Vampire? That she is my mother?

"No! Get the fuck out!" I was suddenly on my feet and furious. "You do not get to come in here and feed me all this bullshit about being my mother and watching over me, protecting me, and then just behave as though that's okay. If you really are my mother, which I don't believe, then where have you been all this time? Why have you never even said hello? Why did you abandon me in the first place? No, I am not having it! You can get the hell out until I have decided how to feel about it all. If you're a mind reader, then I'll guess you'll know when that is!" I pointed to the door and Ana stood slowly.

She smiled at me sadly and looked almost like she would reach out but seemed to think better of it. "I am sorry to have hurt you, Jenna. I will go now, as you wish, but I will continue to watch because you are important to me. When you are ready, I would like to continue our conversation." I blinked and she'd gone, just like before, just simply gone. I slumped into my chair suddenly exhausted.

I sit for the next hour, maybe more, simply staring into the flames. I really don't know how to feel about this revelation. To be fair, I don't even know Ana, this could all be some ruse to manipulate me. Then I rationalise that actually she has asked nothing from me but tea and has never offered even the hint of a threat. The fire spits, and for a second, bright blue flames reach upwards. I am out of my chair and grabbing a coat for appearances immediately as I remember, I am supposed to be meeting Luc.

14

Awkward Moments

Luc

"Lugus!"

"Mum, please. You know I prefer Luc. Lugus sounds like some nasty bodily fluid."

"It does not, you ungrateful little trout. The good god, Lugus, was a mighty warrior, I can only hope you'll be strong enough, my boy."

I really don't know what to say to that, whether my mum is suggesting I'm a disappointment, a pansy, or indeed if she's just as mad as a box of frogs. I decide it's probably the latter and try to edge round her.

"Where do you think you are going, boy? I need you."

"I'm meeting someone, Mum, I gotta get ready."

"Are you indeed, boy? Is this someone a she?"

I sigh and nod again, trying to edge away before my mum goes off about safety and morals, but when she says nothing and reaches out her hand to catch mine; I stop, giving her a quizzical look.

My mum is a tiny woman, and she pulls me down towards her so she can place her hand across my forehead, as though I'm a child with a cold. I quirk an eyebrow and she takes my chin and stares into my eyes, like she's trying to discover the meaning of life.

"She's on your mind all the time, isn't she, boy? Makes you feel whole?"

"Yes, Mum, she really does."

"How have you been feeling in yourself, Son?"

"I'm not sick, Mum, if that's what you mean."

"It's chilly out, do you feel the cold?" Mum asks at random

I'm a little bit thrown by her change of subject, and affirm that no, I don't really feel cold. That thought only bothers me slightly, as I get ready and notice that it snowed last night. Mum walks away from me, shaking her head and continues to go on about finding the book.

———

Later, sitting in yet another wine bar, I realize that we always meet in public places, and that's never really seemed odd to me until now. I suppose it's because she's late, and I've had time to sit and wonder what the hell we are doing. I really can't tell if she likes me, likes me, or if she considers me a friend. Which of course sets me to wondering if I could handle being friend-zoned by Jenna. If I am completely honest with myself, I really don't think I can. Jenna is coming to mean everything to me, and I haven't even held her hand since that night in the hospital. It really is the weirdest thing; she always seems so tense when we're alone. Well, not that we've been properly alone. I mean like not right in the thick of it, surrounded by people. She doesn't seem to want to do private, and I wonder again if maybe she's just killing time with me, or more likely doesn't see me as anything other than a friend. She is almost an hour late now, and I think it's really time for me to give up. I don't think she's coming, so I stand to walk back to the bus stop, when suddenly she's in front of me. She looks flustered and her hair is all over, like she's run down the high street. "Jeez, you scared the bejesus out of me!" I exclaim in shock

For some reason, that remark seems to strike her as really amusing and she giggles for the first time. I can't even tell you what that sound does to me. I just know that I don't want to be only friends.

"Luc, I am so sorry. I got, well, something came up. Were you leaving?" she asks, and I don't think I'm imagining the hurt in her eyes

"Not likely," I reply quickly, "just popping to the loo. Sit, I'll be right back."

She sits as I move away to dutifully pretend to visit the bathroom, and on the way back, I buy her a glass of wine from the bar. I don't actually think she ever touches the wine, but it's what she always orders. As I return to the table, she seems preoccupied and is staring into the distance, so much so that she starts as I sit down.

As she looks up, I can see barely concealed anguish in her eyes. "Luc, do you know your parents?"

"Yes, I still live with my mum, actually. I don't really remember my dad though. He died when I was little."

"I'm sorry, I didn't know."

"Of course you didn't, how would you? Oh I know, you've been stalking me, haven't you? You just can't keep away," I joke, trying to ease her melancholy. It works a little as her lips tilt, just a bit. Feeling emboldened, I reach for her hand and register somewhere in my mind that my hands are much warmer than hers. She looks down at our hands and then back to my face, frowning slightly

"Hey, it's okay. Whatever it is you can tell me, or not. It's your call. Okay?" She stares into my face, and I swear the whole world just fell away. Her eyes are the prettiest shade of violet, and it feels as though if I sit here long enough; I could literally find all the answers to life's mystery inside them.

"Your eyes are really blue, Luc" she comments. I mumble something about being the freak in the family, and her stance seems to change, like she's intrigued by something and trying not to be obvious. She wants to know what I mean by that. I'm working out how best to explain, and I know it's going to sound weird. The thing is, blue eyes are not really that unusual, except in my family. I am literally the only one with blues in a whole family of greys, greens and browns. For some reason, that has always struck me as odd, even though I can't really explain why. I just feel different. Sometimes I just know things that I have no business knowing, or indeed, no interest in knowing. Like I know my mum is waiting, for what I don't know, but she's waiting. Sometimes patiently and sometimes not so patiently. I also know it has something to do with me. She is waiting for me to do something, or say something, but she hasn't pushed for anything, even information about Jenna, for ages. Which come to think of it is quite unusual.

As my thoughts return to the here and now, Jenna looks again at my hand holding hers and she smiles, just a little bit, and squeezes back gently. It is such a small gesture, but I feel my spirits lift with the possibility that she likes me, too.

Jenna goes on to tell me that she has never known her parents and that she was largely raised by a woman called Camilla, whom she hasn't seen for years. She skirts round why that is by saying that people change, but it's not always a good thing. She explains that she has no memories of life before she was taken in by the Camilla woman and that it bothers her. She doesn't know who she is anymore. She feels as though her life is coming to some kind of junction, where everything will change for better or worse, and that she has no control over any of it.

I sit, holding Jenna's hand, and listening to her pouring out her pain to me, and I cannot think of a single place I would rather be. The only change I would make in the world, at this moment, is the suffering I can see etched in those beautiful violet eyes. "You know, Jenna, memories are subjective. They are coloured by the emotions of the person that's remembering, and those emotions change over time and telling. Maybe one day, you'll be able to relate this story again and it won't hurt so much. Maybe there is a really good reason that the memories are gone for now, sometimes they come back when you are ready and strong enough to deal with what is there."

"Surely that means that they must be horrific, or at least incredibly painful, for me to have locked them away so tight?"

"But that might not be for the reasons you think. As an adult, your logic is that something must be terrifying or horrifying to be that bad, but to a child; simply losing someone they care about can trigger an emotional lockdown. I don't obviously know what happened to you, but if I can help you in any way to open and walk through those doors, then you can count on me." I squeeze her hand again, which remarkably, she hasn't pulled away yet, and hope that she will let me help her. I have no idea truly what could cause such memory loss, but it can't be so terrible that I would want to run from her, surely?

She looks sad then and gives me a half-hearted smile.

"Luc, thank you. I really appreciate the offer, but I suspect, that what I might find behind those doors, would cause braver souls than you or I to flee. Why else would they be locked away?" Truly I have no very good answer to that and we sit in silence for a while.

15

Reunion

Ana

"The children have met, you know," the old lady starts when I speak. I feel marginally bad for appearing as I have, but she's used to it and tougher than she looks. She snorts when she sees me

"I thought as much, he's not feeling the cold and has had his head up his arse, for weeks now. Boy doesn't know if he's Arthur or Martha half the time!"

I still struggle with this woman's speech patterns, even after watching all these years. So I just nod sagely in agreement and she smirks at me. "No idea what I said, have you? Ha! Some all-knowing, wise woman you are. Have you stolen my bloody book? Can't find it anywhere!"

"Lillith, you know, good and well, I do not claim to know everything. Just most things, and yes, of course I have your book. I didn't want you losing it!"

"Oh, ye of little faith, I have been watching over the boy and the book for generations, as well you know. I'm not quite as mad as you seem to think."

Laughing, I hand Lillith her precious book. "Yes, crone, I am well aware who you really are and am thankful for it. The boy couldn't have had a better guardian."

"Is the girl strong enough?"

"Only time will tell now, Lillith, but what we do know is that they'll be stronger now that they have each other. I also have this for you..." I opened my hand and dropped the topaz pendant into hers.

She gasps, looking stunned. "Ana! You found it? Where did you find it? I thought it was gone for always." She looks close to tears now, and I reach out to her half-expecting for her to flinch away as she has before. This time, however, she leans towards me and I am able to embrace my sister, as I have not done for centuries.

Although our brothers had argued, we had never wanted to and yet we'd been loyal to them and drifted apart. When telling Jenna about our beginnings, I had deliberately left out my sister's choice to follow her son through his mortality. She'd been devastated to find he did not share our longevity, and so followed him through bearing him as an infant time and again, guiding his spiritual journey to build the strength and resilience he would need to survive what was to come. We both stood to lose our children, should we fail now, and as one mother to another we clung together for support.

16

Meeting Mum

Luc

As we walk through the town, I keep Jenna's hand. She doesn't seem to mind and I simply can't bring myself to let go. I worry that she always feels cold and wonder if she is unwell. I've gotten the feeling that Jenna doesn't work but we've never gone into it as she seems reluctant. I can't just ignore my concerns anymore, and so I start out with a lunch invitation.

"Oh, thank you but I really can't tomorrow, I have commitments." She leaves that hanging and now my choice is to push or leave it vague, as usual. I decide that I am in far too deep to ignore it anymore and throw caution to the wind.

"Why is it I hardly ever see you during the day?" I have

clearly caught her off guard and she stops to look at me. "What?"

"You never come out when the sun is bright. You look pale to me, and your hands are so cold. Are you sick?" I am definitely not mistaking the panic that shoots across her expression then, so I take a different tack and move to sit on the nearby bench overlooking the river. "Look, Jenna, I'm worried is all. I...I really like you, and if there is something that you need from me or that I can help with, you just need to say." As I finish the statement, for some reason the hairs on the back of my neck prickle, like a dog raising its hackles. Ignoring the sudden feeling of trepidation, I reach out my hand slowly to cup her cheek, hoping she won't pull away. She looks into my eyes and she looks spooked, like a rabbit in headlights.

"I'm extremely photosensitive," she finally replies, which may actually be the furthest thing from my mind in this somewhat intense moment.

"Right, okay."

"And...I have poor circulation," she continues, sounding like she is plucking reasons from the air.

"Jenna, please, you don't have to explain yourself, but I worry, more than I probably should. I need to know that you're okay, and if you are not okay, then can I help? How does the photosensitivity effect you?"

She looks like she has never been asked such a straightforward question before and has to prepare her thoughts before replying. "The sun makes me feel weak and nauseous, so I prefer to stay indoors on bright days."

I have trouble with this, never being able to enjoy the sun seems terribly sad to me, and the first words out of my mouth are, "Wow! That sucks!"

Jenna looks highly amused by my choice of words and replies, "Yes, it does indeed suck," whilst clearly trying not to laugh.

Smiling now at my idiocy, I say, "Let me at least feed you. You always decline dinner or lunch, and I've never seen you eat. That worries me, too"

"It's very common that a girl won't eat in front of a new love interest."

"Is that what I am?"

"I'm still trying to decide." I smile as she looks up at me, and stupidly my heart feels like it's going to flip-flop right out of my chest in a minute

"You look hungry though."

"I am"

"So let's get something to eat."

"Tempting, but not a great idea. I have very specific dietary needs."

"I'm sure I could help you find what you need," I retort, rather determined now to have her concede to my need to provide and protect.

Again my choice of words seems to cause her amusement, and she stifles it badly to reply, "I'm certain that you probably could, love, but honestly I am fine for now. It is getting late though, won't your mum be worrying?"

It suddenly doesn't matter to me that she hasn't really answered my questions or that she won't let me buy dinner again. She called me, love, whether she meant to or not, and my insides feel like they might actually be made of jelly. She stands and reaches down for my hand, while I am staring at her like a fool. She smirks, seeming to know she's thrown me off course, and says, "Come on, Lost Boy, I'll walk you home."

As we walk back through the city, I realize that I am not leading, but we are in fact heading in the right direction. "Jenna, are you actually my stalker?"

"Would that be a good thing or a bad thing?" she asks, smirking back at me.

"Well, I think that could be quite a weird thing if you're planning on murdering me, or it could be cool that I have my very own stalker. Or it could just be creepy?" I phrase the last as a question and look to her for an answer, with one eyebrow raised.

She stops, reaching up to press it back down, smiles and fails to look hurt. "Actually, I was remembering from when you came out of hospital, I just assumed you would let me know if we were going the wrong way..." Turning, she starts walking again, in the right direction as before.

We arrive before long in the little street where I have lived with my mum for years, and I really don't want to go home just yet. It occurs to me how very ungentlemanly it is for me to allow her to walk me home, and then leave her to find her own way, and I'm thrilled to have a reason to carry on. I am a bit chilly though so I decide a jacket might be in order as we pass by.

"Jenna, I can't leave you to walk home alone. Come in and let me fetch a jacket, and then I can walk you back. It'll make me feel better." I add the last expecting her to argue, as usual, that she is in fact capable and always managed before we met, to which I obviously always respond by reminding her of Robbie and the night we met.

That had been a close call if ever there was one. I had read in the newspaper, a few days later; not only had Robbie been found dead that night, but the investigation into his sudden and unexplained death had resulted in him being tied to dozens of rape and murder cases across the UK. There was a huge amount of speculation around his murder, and one of my favourite theories held that he'd been killed by some kind of vigilante as a direct result of his own misdeeds. It had haunted me ever since, that Jenna might have been his next target. That particular concern, however, is usually met with a mysterious smile that I am determined I will understand one day. To my surprise, she just agrees quietly and suggests that she should wait outside, in case we disturb my mother. Before we get a chance to debate this further, the front door is flung open and my mother can be seen outlined against the hallway light.

"Come on then, your heating the street!" she squawks, as is her way when she is in a demanding mood, and I have the strangest feeling that she was waiting for us.

"I was just stopping for a jacket."

"Yes, yes, but come inside. No point standing here with the door open," she yells amiably.

"Mum, you opened the door," I reply before noticing that Jenna is locked into a staring match with my mum that should terrify me. They seem to be sizing each other up and for some reason that leaves me a little uneasy. Vaguely I wonder who would win if these two women seriously got into it.

Suddenly Jenna breaks the tension by pulling me forward. "Come on, Luc, we're heating the street!" With that I am pulled through my own front door into the warmth of home.

My mum is instantly in 'fuss over a guest' mode, and I watch as Jenna allows herself to be ushered into the living room. It feels quite pivotal, this random meeting, but I guess that's just nerves since I know Jenna means more to me than any other girl I have introduced to Mum. Come to think of it, I am not even sure that I have brought a girl home before. My mum can be a bit of an old crone. I proceed up the stairs, listening to the muted rumble of their voices while I go to fetch a jacket.

____

Jenna

For some reason, I don't really want to enter the house that Luc lives in with his mother, like I really, really don't want to go in there. It's almost like a compulsion or ward but that can't be, can it? Luc is certainly special but I don't sense a magical ability. I am just suggesting that I should stay outside when Luc's mother opens the front door wide, illuminating the street where we are standing and invites us both inside. The unpleasant feeling of the house dissipates almost instantly, when she offers me the invitation and I look at the small woman again properly. We stand at opposite ends of her garden path, and yet I can feel immediately the power contained in her small frame. She feels to me like a force of nature, but I am almost certain that should she not wish to be known, she could cloak very well. This indicates to me that she is ready to be known, or at least recognised, and that for the moment at least, I am welcome in her company. Curious now, I tug gently on Luc's hand. I need to know more about this woman and I certainly won't find the answers out here. Upon entering the hallway, she takes my hand. I am surprised when there are no sparks; such is the power I feel from her. She leads me into a quaint little living room with a squashy, well-loved sofa and matching chair. There seems to be knick-knacks and ornaments cluttering every surface and a very homey and safe feel to the room. Luc's mother, Lillith, sits me on the sofa and then steps back as though to appraise me. Her eyes narrow, and I feel suddenly foolish for putting myself essentially at her mercy.

"Does he know?"

"Excuse me?"

"My boy, does he know what you are yet?" demands Lillith, getting in my face.

"Er, no."

"Right, best you tell him then, girly, because it'll be quite the shock. He'll need time to process, and I'll not tolerate you feeding here. You do what you need to do elsewhere and we'll get on just fine!" With that she stalks out of the room for all the world like she is six foot tall and solid built. Her stride, in that moment, is completely at odds with the image she presents of a tiny, little aged woman looking out for her adult son.

I am struck by several thoughts in that moment. First, she knew me for the creature I am, instantly and without doubt. Second, is that this, in itself, is not a problem to her, but that I have not told Luc my life story, or what I know of it, is a problem. Following close behind those thoughts is the logic that Lillith is definitely not all she presents herself to be, and I wonder if I should consider her a threat. I jump when she replies, because she has somehow returned to the room without my noticing and is responding to the thoughts in my head. Placing down a tea tray, she all but glares at me.

"You should absolutely consider me a threat, girly. If you don't treat my boy right, or don't watch his back effectively, then I'll have your head. I have no doubt that your mother will then have mine, but without my boy, I really don't think I'll care, so there it is!"

I look at her, with surprise clearly written on my face, and the only word I can find is, "Mother?"

Lillith sits down to my right and turns my face towards her. "Show me your eyes, girl. Your true eyes!"

Surprised, I blink away the brown glamour that I wear with everyone except Luc and she smiles then. "That's better, don't hide who you are, Brigit, the world is a better place with you in it. Be proud of who you are, I know your parents are proud as punch." I frown.

"My name is Jenna."

"Aye, child, but it wasn't always." With that mysterious comment she lets me go and we hear Luc coming back down the stairs.

17

Triggered

Jenna

Later, after eventually escaping Luc's mother, we walk along the river, not even in the direction of home. I decide to try and find out a little more about Luc, or more specifically, what he knows of himself and his mother. My suspicion is not a lot. I know he has a lot of respect for the woman who raised him single-handedly for most of his life, but now I am completely sure she is also keeping a lot of secrets. Although I have no desire to come between mother and son, Luc is coming to mean far too much to me, for me to just ignore anything that could hurt or endanger him.

"Luc, where are you and your mother from originally?"

"She goes on about Celtic this and that sometimes, so I

think there must be some Irish in there somewhere, and as I told you before, my actual given name is Lugus after the Celtic god of light, I think..."

"That's a lot to live up to, isn't it?"

"Yeah, I suppose it would be, if I believed in all that stuff," he laughs. "Actually, I have been a bit worried about her recently, but I don't really know why. She seems fine, I just get this feeling that she's watching me all the time, waiting for something, and she's been talking to herself more and more this last couple of months. She goes on and on, muttering to herself about finding the book and what if we can't find it––The storm is coming!" The last is said in such a comical imitation of Lillith that I actually snort in response, which sets Luc to laughing and I am desperately trying not to, in case I malfunction again. This as I am sure you can imagine, is not something that happens to me often, and I am both disgusted and amused that I have done so.

"Do you believe in the gods, Luc? Mythical creatures, all that stuff?" I ask when we stop giggling.

"I don't know, Jenna, I am certain there is a lot more to this world than we know about or can scientifically prove. I am also certain that the universe is far too big a place to be wasted on the likes of us. and that human life and intelligence cannot possibly be the pinnacle of success in such a large place. But what that means in relation to your question...I really don't know."

"Wow! That's more than I was expecting"

"What about you, do you believe?"

"That's actually a different question, or could be, but yes I believe. I believe there are mysteries and origin stories that we will neither ever know nor understand." With that I step to the river's edge and stand looking down into the water. I feel like I have the weight of the world sitting on my shoulders.

Luc

She wrapped her arms around herself, as though for comfort, and hedging my bets; I step up behind her and wrap my arms around hers. She tenses for a second and then relaxes, leaning back into me. We stand like that for a long time, saying nothing but with her seeming to need strength and me offering mine. It feels to me like a very important moment, almost as though, that small choice, to be together now, might hold the power to alter the course of our lives. I think I was about to say something cheesy along those lines, when a voice I thought I had imagined spoke behind us.

"Might I intrude?" Ana asks stepping from the shadows, for all the world like she might have materialized.

Jenna seems unsurprised and sighs as she looks around me. "Since you seem to have done so, does that not make the request somewhat redundant?" Jenna asks in response, as she moves between us.

"Luc dear, nice to see you alive and well," Ana states,

smiling at me, and I must admit at this point my head is kind of swimming. I had absolutely convinced myself that I had imagined this woman in a smoke inhalation and trauma-induced episode. To have her standing here now, and to find that she is obviously acquainted with Jenna, really pickles my thought processes.

"You know each other?" Jenna asks, looking at each of us.

I have no answer for her other than the struck dumb look that I am now wearing. Ana however seems on top form and laughs lightly.

"I think, dearest, that your Luc had imagined me a psychotic episode, an invention of his somewhat traumatized mind. However, Luc dear, I did indeed save your life that night, and I did indeed cause you to move 'magically' from one building to the next. In doing so I did wrench your shoulder, darling, and for that I apologise but I also came and healed you afterwards——not that you knew that. Questions?" She raised one eyebrow and leaned back against the lamppost behind her, crossing her arms as though casually awaiting the next bus.

"Yes, actually," replied Jenna tartly "How exactly is it that you can sneak up on me like you do? That should not be possible and well you know it!"

"That, dearest, is a conversation for another time. Right now I am here to point out what a piss poor job you're doing of opening the doors." Jenna looks both angry and tense now. It gives me a prickling sensation down my spine, quickly followed by a burst of warmth and an excruciating pain in my stomach. I have never in my life felt any pain so bad, and I am only vaguely aware of Jenna catching my arm as I double over. "There you go, much better," Ana commented dryly, and I glance up to catch a small smile. My accusation is cut off, as another pain wracks through me. I started to drift as I hear Ana suggest she take me home and Jenna assert that she can manage.

———————

Jenna

I lift Luc into my arms, mildly grateful that he'd passed out, since I won't have to explain how that is possible. "What the hell did you do to him?" I yell in Ana's face as she tries to help me.

"Nothing, dearest, I swear. Your anger with me has triggered his change and protection response. It would have happened eventually. I just sped up the process."

"Some protection response, how can he protect anyone passed out?" I scoff, sure now that Ana is entirely mad.

"That's only because it's the first time, Trust me, the next time he'll be magnificent!" Ana's eyes twinkle as she makes that assertion, and I am not entirely certain what we are talking about for a moment.

Before I can argue, Ana reaches out to touch both of our arms, and the floor lurches away from under my feet. As I regain my balance, I find myself standing outside Luc's front door and his mother is marching towards me.

"Well, that was quick, did you even get as far as telling him who you are?" she demands, looking at her son in my arms with no surprise or indeed concern. She simply raises her eyebrows and waits for me to respond. When I don't Ana replies from behind me.

"Of course not, she was bumbling along, so I made her angry. He triggered!"

"Aye, that'll do it every time, well bring him in for me. I don't have the strength I used to."

It is my turn to raise an eyebrow in question and Ana just laughs. Lillith, for her part, offers no apology and simply continues up the path. "Well, you know the neighbours are watching and there'll be questions. Come on get inside!"

With that she is gone again, and I follow her into the house with a feeling like I might have fallen down the rabbit hole.

I carry Luc to his bed and sit with him for what feels like hours. He seems to be running far too hot for the sheer lack of concern either of the other women are displaying.

They seem quite happy to sit downstairs, drinking ever more tea, and occasionally coming up to try and convince me that he is fine and to go home. I simply cannot leave him though. I have no idea what to do to help, and so I repeatedly wipe his forehead with a cold flannel and place my hands on the flesh of his arms, head, and torso to try and cool him down. For what little good it is doing, I honestly fear the worst and briefly consider trying to change him before it is too late. Such is my desire to keep him with me for always. I don't attempt it though. I keep reminding myself that I had never had a choice about what I am, but that if he were to join me, Luc should have that choice. He should at least know that vampires exist before facing that decision.

I have the sense that both Lillith and Ana are aware of the turn my thoughts have taken and are desperately trying not to interfere in whatever I decide. I could have listened to their conversation, of course, but I just can't be bothered. Every now and then Luc's body is wracked with more pain and he curls in on himself. Each time, I lower his head back down and hope he will soon wake. He doesn't wake though, instead he suddenly screams as though the hounds of hell are devouring him, and just as suddenly, Ana and Lillith are both beside me. Lillith looking proud and Ana, for some reason, keeps smiling, causing an urge in me to rip her head from her shoulders. She looks at me with a smirk. "You can try, dearest, if you like. Or we could move Luc now. I think it is time."

"Yes, yes!" states Lillith wringing her hands. "We must move him to the basement quickly!"

Before I can really process the weirdness of the exchange, Ana has scooped Luc up, as I had done before. She is following Lillith to the basement, where she lays him gently onto a large bed, in the middle of what at first glance looks like a steel cage. As I moved closer into the room behind them, I realize the bars are coated in silver, and if my heart had any beats left I think it might have stopped in that moment.

Silver is poisonous to most 'mythical' creatures to some degree, but to vampires it is deadly. Were they taking my Luc from me? Just then he screams, and I rush the bars almost gripping them but stopping just short. "What are you doing––he needs help!" I cry in frustration and Lillith shakes her head.

"No, what he needs is time and to be contained until the madness passes, you should probably step back." She herself, and Ana both step back as Luc starts to convulse on the bed. I watch in horror as he twists and turns in his agony, screaming aloud; a terrible sound that begins to take on an eerie, otherworldly quality that holds me in my place more effectively than the threat of silver burns.

Luc has started to howl. As I lean forward to look more closely, I see that his skin is starting to ripple outward as though pushed from the inside. My mind in its already dazed state, from everything that has already happened this night, is slow to catch what my eyes can already see.

I can see that thick fur is rippling across his body and replacing his now very pale skin. I can see that he is physically growing and changing shape. His clothes are ripping to shreds as they become too tight and completely the wrong shape. His nails and teeth are elongating and his face is distorting. I can see all these things but my mind is close to fracture, and I simply cannot not accept that the kind, gentle soul I had considered bringing into my world may, in fact, be a werewolf.

How could he be, they are supposed to be extinct? This cannot be happening! As suddenly as it has come on, this evening it is over and Luc is a fully transformed Alpha Wolf. He is indeed, as promised, quite magnificent. His eyes are the same fantastic blue as before, and his fur is the most beautiful white with rich grey patches. He rears back in his frustrated pacing and throws himself at the bars, yelping immediately and breaking into a howl that brings my cold skin out in goosebumps.

On some level, I am aware of the other women still in the room and watching from the wall, but I cannot take my eyes off Luc's wolf. He could probably destroy me with ease, and yet, I move forward as though pulled by an invisible string. As I move forward, so does Luc, sniffing the air and whining as though pained or lonely. I hear Ana's warning and totally disregard it in that moment, as I stand staring into to the hypnotic eyes of this wolf and willingly push my hand between the bars. Even though I know that logically, he could easily detach my arm. However, he just draws me in and seems as eager for the contact as I am. His nose touches my palm and he whines again, pushing his head under my hand as I bend down and slowly put my other hand through the bars. He looks up into my face as I place my hands on each side of his. The moment feels electric to me; we lock gazes and I stand transfixed, for I don't even know how long.

I am dimly aware that Ana and Lillith are whispering about how amazing it is, and we clearly can't help ourselves. I also hear Lillith comment that she has never seen a newly fledged pup have such self-restraint, that they are usually wild for at least the first three turns. I hear this and clearly register it on some level, but am equally completely unaware of anything but the deep crystal blue of those eyes and suddenly Luc's voice is in my head.

I gasp but reply silently, asking if he is okay.

Luc continues to stare into my eyes and I can hear the anxiety and confusion in his mental voice, "Jenna, what has happened to me?" I reply silently again that I really don't know for sure, but that I feel his mother had known this would happen, since she seemed both unconcerned and unsurprised when I had brought him home. He dipped his head then, in what I take to be a nod of ascent. I feel a wave of anguish from him so strong that I want to take him up in my arms but I cannot, and I know instinctively that Lillith will not unlock the cage this night. Making sure that my skin is covered completely, I sit down as close to the bars as I dare, and Luc joins me on the other side. We sit like this for the rest of the night and I don't even notice when Lillith and Ana withdraw. We simply sit together silently, and I watch over him while he sleeps fitfully, whining as though in anguish often.

18

A Change of Direction

Lillith and Ana sat together in the lounge drinking tea and patiently waiting for the sun to rise and trigger Luc's reverse transformation. Ana kept trying to make light conversation and Lillith kept trying to ignore her——sister stuff really. Until eventually as the sky began to lighten, they both felt the shift as it sent ripples of change through the house. Lillith felt the magical lock release on the cage, and less than a minute later, Jenna and Luc emerged from under the stairs. Luc looked tired and haggard, wearing only a pair of jogging bottoms that Lillith had left at the bottom of the stairs for him. As they entered the room, Jenna spotting an afghan on the sofa, quickly scooped it up, and wrapped it around his shoulders. Luc gave her a grateful smile and then looked at his mother. Lillith for her part held her ground; she looked Luc over then stood to lay her hand on his head, flinching slightly at the heat coming from his skin. "You've questions, I imagine?" Lillith stated, gesturing for Luc to sit and passing him a cup of tea.

"Yeah, you might say that, Mum," replied Luc sarcastically. Feeling his anger roll outward, without thinking, Jenna placed her hand upon his shoulder, he looked up and then placed his hand over hers.

Lillith settled herself back into the armchair with a sigh and asked Luc where he'd like to start. He snorted in response and rather explosively demanded, "How about we start at the part where I turn into a fucking wolf? And not only did you know, but you were clearly waiting for it, and yet you still said nothing! I suppose it slipped your mind?"

"Trust me, Lugus, I have thought of very little else for a very long time; it was always going to happen. What I didn't know was when, and when you're as old as I am, you tend to learn a fairly effective wait and see strategy"

"What has age even got to do with anything? Not only am I supposed to believe that werewolves exist, but that you know all about it from wherever, and that it's okay? That my life is now over with because of some curse? I'm not okay with it, not at all!"

"I think we need to wind back the clock a little. You need to understand what a 'werewolf' is before you start throwing your toys out of your pram, dearie," chimed in Ana. Both Luc and Lillith shot her such identical withering looks that Jenna tried to stifle a laugh and turned her face away.

Ana though, was undeterred and asked Jenna, "Please fetch Lillith's book, dearest, I believe you'll find it on the kitchen table."

Returning, Jenna placed an ancient-looking tome onto Lillith's coffee table with wide eyes and a clear reverence. Even Luc felt the ripples of power emanating from its pages. With a sigh, Lillith sat forward and reached for the book. "I think we should start with the 'Legend of the Werewolf,' as the ancients told it." With that she flicked open the heavy front cover to reveal pages that were not crumbling with age and fading to dust as Jenna and Luc had suspected, but pages made of the highest quality vellum, gleaming with a sheen that would suggest it were bound just yesterday. Luc and Jenna shared a look, whilst Ana clapped her hands like a child at Christmas. Lilith rolled her eyes and began to read.

"In the forests and uplands of Mide there came a time of hardship never before known in the land.

The cattle were diseased and the crops failed for harvest.

The people of Mide saw death coming to their door.

The winter would soon be upon them and it looked to be harsh.

Then over the fell came the lordly stag, bringing his harem as to make a new home.

The stag was soon noted to be gone, but the deer stayed

and the people sent praise to the gods.

They sent praise and blessings to the god, Cernunnos, for bringing his children so the people might eat.

As years passed, the deer stayed in the forests and the people forgot to be thankful.

They grew greedy in their hunting and bothered no more with the raising of cattle.

So it is told that again, the god, Cernunnos, came over the hill, this time wearing the skin of a wolf.

The wolf, it is said, did not eat from the herd but instead protected them and their young.

Some hunts he watched and others he chased away.

Sometimes he made to take a child or babe but never did.

The wise women told stories of the wolf and his lessons to all.

He taught the hunters to take only as need would have.

He taught them respect for the land that provides them.

He taught them to fear for their young as do the woodland creatures.

One day a lion was seen in the hills and the hunters made to protect the village.

It is told that on that day, a man walked from the woods to the hills in view of the village.

None of the people knew the man but that he seemed unafraid and his step did not falter.

They say that when the man reached the lion, a great

wind whipped the leaves into the air.

The man was hidden from the people.

When the leaves settled, the man was no more and in his place was the Great Wolf.

Protector of the herd, and on that day, he fought with the lion.

The wolf fought the lion and the people knew gratitude again.

The Great Wolf not only protected the animals, but the people as well.

The people learned courage from the lion and the wolf.

They learned to take with respect and to protect those in need.

It is said that the Wolf god will one day return."

––––––––––

Luc

When my mother finished her tale, silence prevailed. I honestly didn't know whether to laugh or cry. She was sitting there looking at me like she'd unveiled the answer to life and the universe. If it weren't for the fact that I had spent the night as a wolf, I think I would have feared for her sanity.

That was when it clicked, it was a joke, a really clever joke. I could not talk telepathically with Jenna, and there was no way I had spent the night in the body of a wolf. My mother had finally cracked and had drugged me so I would believe it, too. I started laughing then, and the three women looked at me; two with concern and Ana with barely concealed delight.

I laughed and laughed and even when I realized that nobody else was laughing, I still couldn't stop. Soon I could hardly breathe and I was still unable to stop. Jenna came round and knelt in front of me, saying something about having to help me. She placed her hands on either side of my head, her eyes did a weird flashing thing as she blew directly into my face. Then I simply checked out, whilst my scattered brain tried to piece itself back together.

———

Jenna

When Luc started laughing, I thought I had missed the joke, but then he continued laughing. As his face reddened and he started coughing, I realized he had landed face first in complete hysteria. He seemed completely helpless to control himself, and I was really concerned that if he didn't draw a decent breath soon, he would damage himself. The only thing I could think of was to knock him out, but I didn't want to hurt him, so I knelt in front of him and took his face in my hands. I locked his head from moving and looked deep into his manic, blue, panicked eyes. I flashed my eyes and blew in his face and I felt him relax almost instantly. His body naturally drawing a huge breath as I released him from his madness, and then he slumped forward into my arms.

Lillith was suddenly by my side and we eased Luc back

into the sofa cushions.

"Well," said Ana from behind me, "that was exciting!" She looked thoroughly amused by the whole thing, and I lost it then. Within seconds, I had the crazy 'woman'—since I was unsold on anything she'd said and undecided as to her species—pressed against the wall of the lounge.

"Do you take anything seriously?" I demanded, just barely containing my monster, as my anger awoke her inside me. Ana did look repentant, as I tried to refrain from choking her; she slowly raised her hands to the side as she had that first night in a sign of surrender.

"Jenna, I am sorry. I meant no harm, it just really was a crazy reaction. Most people when introduced to the supernatural go rampaging around trying to kill anything that moves. I think that Lillith will back me on this—that's why we caged him last night, after all." Ana just looked at me as I tried to reason through her words. I knew there was no point to this, but just recently my anger seemed to be so close to the surface, the violence barely concealed, and I realized I had not fed for at least a week. This was not a good situation for me.

Lillith slipped up beside me, and laid a gentle hand on mine, as though to restrain but with no strength behind it. "Jenna, I suspect you don't really understand any of this either, or I am sure you would not be holding Ana's life to ransom. I do not think she meant any harm, it is simply her way. Infuriating though it may be at times. Perhaps, dear, you should feed and then we can go on with this conversation?" She clenched her hand just slightly, but it allowed me the momentum to release my own. Ana returned lightly to her feet, looking no worse for wear and straightened her jacket as I mumbled an apology.

"Think nothing of it, dearest, if anything, it encourages me greatly to see you already so attached. Now with regards to feeding, if you leave the house and travel over the rooftops due east, you will find a child predator that fits your requirements. I believe his plan is now firm enough that he'll catch your attention less than a mile from here." I nodded my thanks and left the house in a rush to meet this Darkness and consume it.

Ana

Lillith sat in her armchair and watched Luc as he restlessly slept. The last fifteen hours had been terribly hard on both his body and mind, and it would take him some time to recover. I sat opposite my sister and waited for her to say something, of course she didn't, since she was more than happy to sit for hours in silence. So I spoke first, as usual, "It's good that she's this protective. The bond will be unbreakable, once it is forged."

Lillith looked as though to ignore me and then sighed almost theatrically. "She's quite the hothead, your Brigit," she said, looking at me sideways and without raising her head.

"She always was," I replied "That's why we sent her away—to learn restraint."

"Well, she has certainly learnt restraint, even if it is still not easy for her. I would question though the logic of having her try to learn restraint surrounded by vampires. Was Camilla really the best role model?"

"Well no, obviously Camilla wasn't the best in that respect, but she did raise and protect my daughter until we stripped her memories because she was growing jealous. She was quite a different leader until we were forced to interfere with her mind."

"So it's your fault she has become a twisted, sadistic Queen of Terror, who built a castle specifically with the torture of human beings in mind?" Lillith asked flatly, as though enquiring after my hairdresser. Lillith looked at me completely straight-faced for a good half a minute before she chuckled, "Don't sweat it, Sis, she was always twisted and sadistic, that's why she took to the life so well. More tea?"

19

Rediscovery

Luc

I slowly drifted towards the surface of my consciousness in a leisurely, half-hearted, sort of way. I registered a soft and melodious voice speaking, and although the words were unclear, the voice made me feel safe. So I allowed myself to drift a little longer, enjoying the rhythm and cadence of the voice. I was troubled though by visions: images of wolves, fires, and a beautiful dark-haired angel, who called to me and held my hand. The angel held my hand and smiled at me, beckoning towards the door. Her violet eyes sparkling with love and reassurance. We walked together, hand in hand towards the old, ivy-covered wooden door, which would not have been out of place in a fairy tale.

As we reached the doorway, I extended my hand to open it. As the door swung open, the voice became clearer and I looked to my angel, confused. She stepped through the doorway and as I followed, I awoke. The voice however continued, clearer even than before.

"...pressure that built, and became unyielding, and eventually there was She.

"She was the Earth Mother, Gaia. Her name, I knew was Lillith."

I opened my eyes, to find myself back on the bed inside my mother's basement cage. Jenna was sitting nearby in an armchair that I didn't recognise, reading aloud from my mother's book. Although I am certain that I made no noise, she paused and looked up. "How's your head?" she asked me when I turned towards her.

"Probably clearer than is advisable," I replied, and she laughed as she closed the book and moved closer to the cage.

"I'm sorry that I had to put you back in there, your mother is unsure if you'll change again tonight or not."

"It wasn't a really trippy dream then?" I asked hopefully

"Sorry, no."

"What were you reading?" I asked, not knowing how else to begin. Jenna looked back at the book before replying that she'd been about to read a piece that claimed to be an origin story from the point of view of the horned god, Cernunnos. It seemed to me as good a starting place as any, and so I asked her if she would continue to read to me since

I had to be here all night. With a small nod and a sad smile, Jenna reached for the book and flipped it open again.

"In the beginning, I knew only darkness and the heat of my own being.

"I knew no boundaries and was entirely unconstrained.

"One day there was a pressure that built, and became unyielding, and eventually there was She.

"She was the Earth Mother, Gaia. Her name, I knew was Lillith.

"She was as strong as myself and seemed to be without boundary. Together we came, my sister and I, into physical form along the cliffs of her land. Lillith was beautiful, her eyes were like pools of ice water and her hair as dark as the great oaks that came to live on her shores. Together we danced under the stars of my brother and in the warmth of my fire.

"Together our happiness was powerful enough to create life. The heat from my sun allowing the trees and flowers to grow strong, in turn the plants aided the creatures to grow equally strong and just as diverse in their form. We rejoiced on meeting our siblings, and for a time, all was well in the world. We loved and danced, we laughed and sang.

"My Lillith though became unhappy, she felt that our sister had more than she. Lillith wanted the waters to pull back from her shore so they could be equals again. I was sent to envoy, but sadly agreement could not be found, and war ensued. The rains and seas buffeted my Lillith and we lost cliffs into the ocean. The winds of course helped to carry the rains and no amount of fire could dry the rivers it created. Lillith was reduced on all sides, and she became sad, losing hope of happiness. She could no longer be fulfilled by the creatures on her earth and winter came upon the world.

"I tried to ease her pain and offered her comfort whenever she would allow, together we watched the world grow cold. We saw the humans rise to be the dominant species on land, and we saw how they loved. Not just an emotional fulfilment but on a physical level. We copied what we learned from the people and soon my Lillith became ill. Such a thing had not happened in our past, and I was in a fervour of worry. She couldn't eat or dance without sickening and I knew fear.

"Then an amazing realization came to us, my Lillith was with babe, just like the human women. I cared for her and brought her fruits. As her time grew closer, I watched the human women birth their children from the eyes of their animals. I learned what I could do to help my love and we waited.

"I was in the body of a wolf the night the child arrived. I had been watching a village near to our home when I heard Lillith cry out for me. I raced to her side and prepared to welcome our child, a child created in physical love. Never before had we created such a child, and I felt that never should we do so again.

"The boy child made his entrance to the world as all

human babes do, screaming with indignation at their abrupt entrance to a cold and unforgiving world. Those first years were very special to us both. The child grew quickly and with strength. He showed a lightness of soul that pleased us both greatly, and as if to celebrate his life, the war with our siblings had ended. We would be ever divided but the fighting was over. We later discovered that they too had birthed a child created in physical love. A girl child, no less, but she was rumoured to have odd eating habits and was difficult to control. Secretly, I hoped that our children would not meet.

"As the child grew, it became more obvious to us that his time seemed to go so fast. He changed so much from day to day, then week to week, and although his growth did slow down to month to month changes, these were still far quicker than we would have expected. In his fifteenth year, the boy became feverish for a period of weeks. I began to suspect that our child may be mortal and in deathly danger. I summoned a wise woman from the village, who looked at me strangely that I should seek her advice, and I wondered briefly if she knew me for what I am. My focus was on Lugus, our light one. Lillith was ever by his side and his fever was no less than before. The wise woman came and declared she would need help; she returned with a man who waved a stick around the boy and chanted to the gods. The old man, I noted, did not recognise me as the woman had, and she soon banished him, calling him a fool.

"The woman came to me then. She asked could I not heal my son, was I not the protector? She told me of the Wolf Man, the god Cernunnos that offered protection and guidance to the creatures of earth. 'Is this not you?' she demanded.

"My only response was to tell the woman I did not know how to help him. She took my hands and drew me towards the child. She laid my hands upon either side of his head, and bid me ease his transition; draw him through. Though I was terrified of what her words could mean, I called to Lugus. The woman laid her hands upon his stomach and forehead and chanted calling to the Faelad—The Wolf Boy she called him.

"The boy was in an agony of pain, his skin burned and rippled and finally, after many hours, the wolf came. He was majestic and regal, an Alpha Wolf with Lillith's crystal blue eyes and a full coat of white and grey.

"Lillith cried that night, the tears of a mother losing her child. We knew then that the boy would live a long life but still be mortal and again I felt fear. I feared for the sanity of my Lillith when the day came to hold his hand and whisper goodbyes, as I had watched so many humans do before. The boy's growth sped for a while and he changed from a tall skinny pup of a boy, into a formidable man of stature, who could mingle in the village with ease.

"The wise woman watched him grow with approval, and I don't think she ever shared our secret with another soul. She would talk with him sometimes, teach him things from her craft, and he grew strong and wise.

"Lillith however was withdrawn and sad again, one day she came to me with a plan.

"She said the wise woman had spoken of other lifetimes that a mortal soul might return to the world after death within another shell. Lillith had decided that she would follow Lugus through his mortal coil, she wished to be his mother, always to guide him and care for him during his younger years and his inevitable transitions.

"Lillith said that with the wise woman's help she was certain she could accomplish the binding of their souls so that they might remain together for their subsequent lives. The wise woman had also said that I should not also follow. She told us a tale of a storm to come and that our beloved son was needed to be a part of the key. The wise woman said that it was my path to remain who I am and to watch. I was to follow Lillith and find her in each lifetime, love her, care for her, and recreate the child, because only then would the binding work and the prophesy come to fulfilment.

"So it was done, the charm was created and the binding accomplished. It was then with sadness that we each stepped upon our separate paths. It was apparently my path to be the watcher, the waiter, the one that sees all things and can enjoy them only briefly. Lillith's path was to die, time and again, for her beloved child, who was born mortal.

"So, Lugus, this is my story and why I am not there to

tell it myself. You see, I cannot stay with Lillith after the birth of the child, as it weakens her body, and she needs her strength to help you grow. You have a great destiny awaiting you, but that is not my tale to tell. If, however, you're reading this now, then the time must be coming. You must be ready for the storm, boy. Only you and your woman can set us all free.

"Your Father, Herne."

As Jenna finished reading, she looked up to meet my gaze. Her eyes held the same confusion that I felt inside as I considered the implied meaning of the words. Could it really be that my mother was some amazing earth goddess, who gave her immortality in order to be with her son? No, surely it was not possible that any of this was true. Yet here I was locked in a cage, having turned into a wolf the night before. I know now that myth and magic do exist and that knowledge had very nearly fractured my mind. Had it not been for Jenna releasing me as she had, I truly believe I might have choked, since I'd been unable to draw breath. At this precise moment, I had no words for Jenna, or indeed anyone else. I simply didn't know what to say. If I thought too hard about the last few months, it became glaringly obvious to me that I should have realized something was off. I was also now certain that Jenna had some part to play in this drama that seemed to be unfolding itself in my lap, but how did she fit in? I kind of briefly hoped she might be the 'your woman' referred to in the book.

I remember suddenly that we had spoken last night through our thoughts and glance at Jenna. She is looking down at the book, still in her hands, but she has a definite smirk on her face. So I shrug physically and apologise in my head, adding, "I can't really help it, you are quite fit, you know." To which she laughs out loud, and I think I might be onto a winner, even if my life does seem to be going to hell in a handbasket.

20

Doubts

Jenna

When Luc finally slept, I quietly left and sought some solitude to gather my thoughts. This thing with Luc was too much, I must break away. Already I was far too attached and his soul was filled with such Light as to burn me if I did not flee. I do not play in the Light; I have always chosen the Darkness. Taking from that Darkness cannot increase my sin to the world. If only I could be such as he, a protector to all who needed help, then maybe I could be forgiven my inherently evil nature. I should burn for my sins, of that I was certain.

"And whom exactly do you think would do such a thing?" asked Ana, appearing behind me as she was want to do. I looked at her coolly and made a mental note to work out her mystery. "Well?" she demanded.

"Well, what?" I replied, pulled from my maudlin thoughts reluctantly.

"Whom do you expect is going to judge you for your 'sins'?" She finger quoted.

"God, I suppose," I replied, gesturing to the front steps of the church opposite.

Ana moved towards me and sat down with me on the roof. "Trust me, dearest, there is no god and no devil that would dare to pass judgement upon you. Some may well think to do so now, but when you have fulfilled your true being, none can stand in opposition unless you let them."

I look at Ana incredulously, I barely know this woman and yet she has basically turned my existence upside down. That had nothing to do with my internal debate about Luc, nope, not at all.

"How exactly do you propose that I will 'fulfil my true being'?" I retort sarcastically, knowing that the answer would be cringe worthy. She didn't disappoint.

"With love," she replies simply, as though this was the most obvious answer in the world.

"Love? You want me to do what now? Start hunting lovers? You surely know that I will not if you're watching so closely."

"Of course not, don't be so literal, dear. I am quite familiar with the life choices you have made. The love of which I speak is your love for Luc, and his love for you in return.”

“I do not love, Ana, I am incapable!”

“Of course you do,” she replies with certainty “You sit here staring at that church, and judging yourself, not because he is inconsequential, but because he matters. Has he not been ever in the forefront of your mind since your meeting? Have you not deliberately walked into Marcus’ trap, rather than expose him to Anthony? Have you not put his health and well-being above your own base needs? You do not do these things for just any mortal, dearest, you do these things for the one soul that sings to your own.”

“Oh, Ana. Stop! How can there possibly be any Light in me? I. AM. VAMPIRE! I am a creature of Darkness, I am evil incarnate. I am incapable of love!”

“Oh, my dearest Jenna. You are SO much more than you believe, and you will make believers of us all.”

“What does that mean?”

“You are what is known as Grey, dearest. You are the embodiment of Darkness but with the lightest of souls. You have the power to wield both the Light and the Darkness, if only you can find the strength to stop it consuming you.”

“That’s why I need Luc?”

“That’s why you need Luc. He is Lugus, The Light One. He is the light to balance your darkness, and you will make each other stronger. The storm is coming, Jenna, and you must both be ready.”

With that Ana stood and leapt into the air. I watched as she transformed seamlessly into a crow and flew away. Ana had really told me nothing new, well not anything that made sense to me right now anyway. What I had realized was that no matter how honourable I wanted to be in leaving Luc's life uninterrupted, it was already too late. He was now forever changed after his transformation yesterday, and so noble intentions or not, there was really now no reason for me to not be with him, if that's what he wanted. He was now a supernatural being too, so why not?

If I was being completely honest with myself, I really didn't need a reason to stay, I was just looking for one to ease my own conscience. However, if I intended to remain a part of Luc's life, I had better be honest about what I was. Discovering who I was and where I had come from would have to come later, or maybe he might help me find the truths that had been kept from me these past centuries. At least I had solved the mystery of Ana's uncanny ability to follow me undetected and turn up everywhere, her ability to shapeshift had slipped my mind until now.

I decided to walk back to Luc's house since I was in no particular hurry. The sky was clear for once, and as I walked through the park, I spotted an apple tree that was struggling in the city air. Climbing it, I sat looking to the stars. If Ana's tale from my study could be believed, then she was my mother and somewhere out there was my father. According to her story, he was the god of air. I wasn't really sure what any of this was going to mean to me, going forward, but I think I'd gotten off lightly compared to the revelations that Luc was working through. At least I was already acquainted with my monster and we had a pretty good working relationship. Luc still had all of that to work through, on top of everything else he had discovered, and everything I would still need to reveal to him.

Did I believe in one true god as taught by the Christian church? I didn't really think so, I rather suspected that my habit of berating myself whilst sitting on church roofs was more about who I was, than who the creator might be. Also, did it really matter what some all-powerful stranger thought of me when clearly I hated myself anyway. I had a lot to work through it would seem, but I think first I had some things to explain to Luc and to decide how I felt about Ana claiming to be my mother.

Ana

I watched as Jenna descended her apple tree and started back in the direction of Lillith's house. I was just thinking to follow when a voice startled me.

"How is she holding up? It's a lot to take in!" Arren stepped from the shadows and my transformation from crow to goddess was instant. My feathers of deepest black morphing like shadows in to a full-length gown of satin. I always did favour the theatrical when with my Arren and now was no exception. "This face," I said, touching his cheek reverently like I had not been able to in so long. "How can you be here?" I asked, even as I snaked my arms around his waist to draw him closer. "I am bid run an errand but I have this night for us"

"You do not wish to spend it with your daughter?"

"There is plenty of time, she does not know me yet for who I truly am." He leaned down and kissed me and that was all it took.

21

Time for Truth

Lillith

After Jenna left, I dared to visit Lugus. We had not been alone since his transformation, and there were things I needed to share with him alone. I had overheard Jenna reading his father's letter earlier in the evening, and I had no doubt that there would be questions for me now.

As I entered, I could see Luc in profile, and I noted that the physical changes were taking hold already. Where my son had ever been slight of build, with an almost gaunt and angular face, now he looked far healthier and more like his father than any of his previous incarnations had achieved.

I need not ask after his feelings for Jenna since the proof was writing itself literally into the lines and contours of his being. Luc stirred, moaning and muttering something incomprehensible about fire, and I didn't have the heart to wake him. Instead I sat in the chair I had brought for Jenna, simply watching.

Fire! Lugus had always dreamed of fire but only in this lifetime had he ever pursued that fascination into his work. Fathered by the god of sun, fire, and fertility, it was no surprise that flames both fascinated him and terrified him equally. Soon I noticed that the pattern of Luc's breathing had increased, and so I left to make tea. Upon returning, I found Luc awake and likely as ready for this little chat as either of us ever would be. Looking up as I entered, I could see the wolf behind his eyes. Luc, however, although weary and wary looking, seemed to have good control over himself. Still I approached slowly and pushed the tea through the bars with extreme caution, so as to cause no alarm to the barely contained alpha I could sense pacing just below the surface.

"Thanks, Mum," Luc said, breaking the somewhat awkward silence we had fallen into and I grasped that as an opener.

"Do you hunger, Lugus?" I enquired.

"Hunger? Since when is that the right word?"

"Since your wolf made himself known to you," I replied without missing a beat.

"Oh! No, I...We? Just no, Mum, it's fine," Luc replied, shaking his head with confusion in his eyes. I perched on the edge of the armchair again, grasping my cup like some kind of lifeline. Now that the time had come, I had no idea how to begin. Strangely it was Luc that took the first step.

"You don't look like her," he stated, and I looked at him confused. "

Well, no. Jenna is quite the unique individual..." I started to reply.

"No, you don't look like the Lillith in the book," Luc clarified and I sighed.

"Yes, well part of mortality is apparently living in whichever physical form you are assigned upon reincarnation. I have been all shapes and sizes over the centuries. Never with blue eyes though strangely, and yet, you, seem to have blue eyes, in every lifetime..." I faded off, remembering. So distracted was I that it was some moments before I realized Luc had said nothing and was simply staring at me.

"What's wrong?" I demanded, panicked although I didn't know why.

"Are you saying that this has happened before?" Luc was now frowning so deeply that I expected the line might become fixed before this night was through.

"Of course this has happened before, did Jenna not read you the letter?" I asked, confused now. I was certain I had heard her speaking our story aloud earlier. Luc continued to frown and stare at me with such a look of stubborn incredulity that I was struck by memories of him as a child, indignant, that he should be allowed more sweets or a later bedtime. An unexpected tear squeezed itself from my eye to roll silently down my cheek, leaving its sleek silvery calling card behind to give me and my blasted emotions away. Spotting it, Luc scoffed, suddenly angry with me, demanding to know why I cried. Was it my life that was over? Had I been lied to everyday of my life? Was it me locked in a silver cage?

In that moment, faced by his passionate feelings of betrayal, I had no words to offer and no advice to impart. Dozens of times over the centuries we had been through his change, dealt with the facts, moved on, and coped. Never before had there been such anger and passion behind his questions, and selfishly, I wanted to flee, to escape this place and his accusatory glare. Luc had his back to me now and I hovered, wanting to run, to leave Ana and Jenna to pick up the pieces, rather than face this judgement. His shoulders slumped slowly as he battled his anger, and I lowered myself gently but determinedly into the chair. I owed him this much, and if I lost him with the truthful telling this time...Well, that was probably how it had to be, since this time was playing out differently. I suspected that was Jenna's doing one way or the other.

As I waited for Luc, I leaned back in the chair, reflecting that many things were different this time. The most obvious being that Luc sat before me in his human form, struggling to, but succeeding in, containing his wolf only the second day after his first transition. Usually the first change saw him howling and throwing himself at the bars of the cage in desperation to escape and feed for at least three nights, usually four. There had been no real rages and no escape attempts thus far, last night Jenna had even dared to touch his wolf without losing a limb.

Always before when the change came, we talked, I explained, then we packed up our belongings and disappeared, living out our days in seclusion. Somewhere that the alpha could feel safe and know peace. This time was already different as to make me suspect that there may not be a next time. This time I had now with my son was, I felt, drawing to its conclusion and that this particular path might be at an end.

I felt sorrow then for the boy child. I would not raise again, and I hoped that I had done my job of subconsciously preparing him well. My failure in this single task would likely cost many lives, including his and my own. I fervently hoped he was ready.

Luc turned his head slightly and seeing me still there sighed deeply. "So, we have been here and done this all before? Logically I guess it didn't end well, since we're getting a do over!" Luc turned to face me, and again I was awed by the control he had already achieved. "As you said, Jenna read me the letter, now I think it's time you explained what came after..." Luc raised a brow, daring me to refuse and instead I nodded. He needed to know if he was going to be ready, and he needed to be ready because, for the first time in centuries, the game board was moving differently, which surely meant the storm was coming.

"As you already know, your father brought the wise woman from the village to help us, when you became ill. Little did we know at the time how different our whole outlook would be within a few weeks. After your first transition, the wise woman became a near permanent fixture in our lives. She helped me to see the positives of this change, and she helped you learn to control your wilder instincts. Your father too was some help in that respect, since he was able to change his form and had already spent some time as a wolf. However, being a man in wolf's clothing meant he didn't have the same urges and instincts as your wolf. So I don't think he ever truly understood your struggles.

"It became increasingly obvious that although your lifetime would be long, it would indeed end of some natural cause if not before, unlike ours which seemed indefinite. Again, it was the wise woman who helped me through the reality of the situation. Since she was able to see more objectively than I, it was she who concocted the idea of binding our souls to each other, but also to the mortal realm itself, so that we might return time and again. It should theoretically allow me to be your mother in each lifetime, allowing me to prepare you for your final test.

"I asked the wise woman what she meant by that and she couldn't or wouldn't tell me at that time, she would say only that the storm would come and you must be ready. That first lifetime was good, apart from the bumpy start, and we enjoyed being a family as long as we could. We had no secrets, and you understood all that had gone before, and we made our decisions as a team. Slowly though your body began to age; we could tell that you had entered into the winter of your life. I hoped with all my soul that the binding would work in the way that it should. It was my understanding that when you died, my own life would 'end' shortly thereafter, and we would enter the waiting place together. I hadn't really considered the mechanics more than that I just knew that I needed to follow you. When the time came though, it could not have been more shocking to me.

"Your first death came one cold winter's night, by then you were an old man, whereas your father and I had not aged. Your bones had been stiff with arthritis for years already, and your hair was as white as the hoar frost coating the ground. We sat with you, and I held your hand, listening to the slowing of your heart and the rattling hiss of your final breaths. I looked to your father, who had tears in his eyes, and then slowly your eyes fluttered closed and your chest stilled. Then I knew only darkness and the touch of your hand as it had not felt for decades.

"We remained in the dark place for time untold, waiting and hoping, clinging to one another, until I opened my eyes. I awoke to find myself a young and nubile woman, in the spring of her lifetime. She was a beautiful creature, with green eyes and shocking orange hair, and she stood in a garden of sorts, surrounded by flowers and trees. I looked about me with both wonder and worry as I tried to imagine what had happened, and then I saw her. The wise woman from our village. The passage of your lifetime alone should have made this meeting impossible, and yet here she was, beckoning for me to follow. Follow I did of course, and I came to a place where your father was awaiting her return. He looked from her to me in confusion at first, until she began to explain. I had been placed in this body to fulfil the next chapter, this human would conceive a child, and that child would bear your soul.

"It was then that I realized the wise woman was no mere awakened human but a supernatural of some kind. Why this had not occurred to me before, I know not. But for her to have fooled Herne and myself, she must be more powerful even than we together could be. I felt fear then, that we had allowed her to dictate our future for her own ends, and as I had these thoughts, she looked to me and laughed. She told us that you were the key and that you were needed to open the door. She said that one would come who could tame your beast and unlock your immortality, and that only then could I be free of my self-imposed sentence.

"Until then I would be placed, time and again, into the body of a maiden whose time to conceive was near, and that in the body of that maiden; I would bear you again as a child. She assured me that Herne knew how to find me when each time came, but that he could not stay after the child was born, as it would age this body too quickly. It was then that I realized that I had committed myself to a life as a lone mother, not just once, but over and over until an undetermined point in the future. What we would be preparing for, or when it might come, was an unknown quantity, and as such, would be difficult to plan for, but plan and prepare we must. Apparently the world was counting on us.

"Since that time, we have lived dozens of lifetimes together, always comes the change and the time for me to tell you the truth. Usually you are unmanageable for the first three or four days over the first change and need to be contained for the first two or three transitions. After that, we can usually talk through everything, set the escape plan in motion, and then move somewhere quiet to live out our days. With each lifetime, I have tried to steer you in different directions so that subconsciously you can learn the world with as much variety and colour as possible.

"Each time I have taken a new form, the wise woman has come to me, imparting what knowledge she felt appropriate to help guide me. Over the years, I have ascertained that there is a prophesy to which she thinks you are the key and that all this 'preparation' is needed so that you might survive the reckoning and become your true self. She could not tell me what that might mean for me, whether I would return to myself or perish with the severed connection. I have planned as though I am to survive and I simply hope I am right.

"Over the centuries, I have perfected the escape plan to the point where it is almost second nature to me now. For example, it has already been initiated, you are currently away from work, seriously ill, and within a few weeks you will die." I looked up to see Luc staring at me with undisguised shock.

"I am going to die?" he demanded, looking alarmed and close to panic, and I instantly realized my mistake.

"No, no dying, I promise. As a wolf though, Luc, there will be certain times that you are unable to work and there will forever now be the possibility that a situation or event might trigger a change. Therefore, steps have already been taken that will lead to your eventual death from some obscure but non-communicable disease. That way there are no awkward questions from people that knew you before, but of course we will have to leave town. Financial arrangements have always been in place, along with secondary ID so that you can still travel as needed." Luc looked no less shocked or alarmed than before, which confused me completely. He frowned, raising his hand, indicating it seemed, that I should give him a moment to process.

The silence between us stretched and I could only imagine the thoughts that must be tying him up in knots. Eventually, he looked at me and stood, approaching the bars slowly, never breaking eye contact as though locked in a silent battle of wills with a challenger. He stopped mere millimetres from the silver and stared at me without blinking or moving. "You will not force me to leave Jenna behind!" he stated in such a firm tone, as to brook no argument, and I sighed in relief. Of all the demands or complaints I had envisaged having to work around, this one I could happily promise to adhere to.

"From what I can work out, my son, I believe she may be the other half of the key. Only the two of you can decide that, however, and as such I would not dare to interfere. I can only tell you that you must do as you feel, follow your heart, and you'll know what is right. You must leave town though, on that I must insist, whether with me or with her is entirely up to you." Luc's shoulders dropped with his relief and he nodded minutely to indicate that he understood. Luc went to turn away and I caught his attention by lifting the pendent into the air from my pocket. "I need to give you this, Lugus," I said simply, rising from my seat to hand it through the bars. He winced slightly at the burn as I laid it reverently in his palm, but he said nothing. It recognised him soon enough and ceased to defend itself. Luc raised his eyes to mine, the question clear as I returned to my seat.

"It was given to me by your father, upon your first birth. It holds the core of our conjoined powers, and you will need it if the time really is coming. You should protect it with your life, in fact protect it with hers. I suspect that will soon mean more to you than your own does." Luc was staring at the pendent with awe in his eyes; it seemed to have completely enchanted him. I tried to see it as he was, for the first time, and I could understand the fascination. It was made of sterling silver and was shaped to represent a goddess with raised arms. The large heart-shaped fire topaz placed to represent wide childbearing hips and a love for all creatures. The smaller oval shaped citrine perfectly placed to represent beauty and emotional intelligence. It truly was a thing of beauty and I had proudly worn it for many decades. But it was time for it to move on, the wise woman, whoever she really was, had led me to believe that Luc would have a great need of this soon.

Luc looked to me with that awe still clearly written on his face and a question in his eyes. "Mum, I can't take this if it's yours from my father." He made to hand the pendant back and I held up my hand.

"Luc, your life and success are far more important to me than a pretty bauble. I am hoping that with your success, I will be restored and your father and I can be reunited, if not and I should perish, then I will not need it anyway. Keep it or give it to Jenna, as you wish. The pendant and its magic are now yours." And so saying the pendent burned with white light at that moment, and Luc gasped, as the glow seemed to pulse and move through the pendent and into his hand, traveling up his arm. Within moments it was over, but not before Luc's entire person had flared white-hot as though it might combust. We stood staring at each other in shocked silence, and I knew without doubt that the time really was coming. If Luc should not survive this test then there would be no second chance. I gazed upon my son, feeling as though the world were literally hanging in the balance.

"Well, that was different," he stated in his characteristic way, making light when things were too serious, and I laughed. What else could I do?

22

Honesty

Jenna

As I approached Lillith's door, it clicked open to allow me entrance, and I noted that whatever latent magic Lillith had held onto during her time of watching; it seemed to be increasing now that Luc had begun his transition. I wondered if she would soon reveal her true self to us and promptly decided not to ask when I caught sight of her face. "What has happened?" I asked in a panic "Is he okay?"

"Yes, he's okay, girly, but what have you done to him? He didn't change last night at all. It's almost as though the first change never happened. He should be wailing and unmanageable for three or four days, but he's just sitting there. Waiting for you to go on talking to him." She eyed me suspiciously, as though I had in some way enchanted her son and enslaved his wolf, neither of which were things I knew how to do. Lillith quirked an eyebrow and huffed off towards the kitchen, I guess she didn't believe me then. I headed down to the basement to find Luc sitting on his bed, as Lillith had stated, which he had moved closer to my chair. He was flicking idly through some innocuous looking paperback, and I suspected that he was again not allowed hands on with the history tome. He looked up, and as our eyes met, I felt the strangest fluttering sensation and Ana's word sought my attention.

She was convinced that I loved this man, that I was capable of loving this man. I didn't know how to feel about that. I do know that I had never felt such a sensation inside, or that any such sensation was possible to me, and my mind reached out to Lillith's increased magic. I drew in a steadying breath and sat on the floor next to the bars of Luc's cage. "Luc, I have something to tell you and it may come as a bit of a surprise." He came and sat opposite me and reached through for my hands, seeming to be careful not to brush my skin on the bars. He seemed to know I was reluctant to touch them. I realized he'd not only had a long time to sit thinking, but also a fair amount of time without me here, and I wondered what his mother might have told him.

"Are you going to tell me where you fit into all this crazy?" Luc asked, with what could only be hope in his eyes.

"What do you mean?" I asked unsure.

"Well, look, I turned into a wolf and you sat with me all night. You read me a story from a history book that implied my mother is Gaia, and my father is the horned god, Cernunnos. Ana defies all explanation, as far as I'm concerned. Although you look as surprised as I feel at these revelations, you don't look in the slightest bit freaked out—unlike me. So I guess what I really want to know is, who or what are you, and whether any of this has changed the direction I think we were heading before it happened?" Luc was still holding my hands as he finished speaking, and he gently squeezed them now in encouragement. I looked into Luc's beautiful blue eyes, and what I saw shining back at me was complete trust. This beautiful Light soul clearly had made up his own mind, as to what I might be in the realm of supernatural, and had also decided it didn't matter. I wondered if it would, and I took a deep and entirely unnecessary breath.

"Luc, I am a vampire," I told him, looking down so as not to witness the rejection on his face.

He was still holding my hands in the absolute silence that followed my declaration of being essentially pure evil. I was certain that he was trying to work out how to remove his hands before I did. I decided to let him off lightly and tried to disengage, but he just squeezed my fingers in response. Releasing my left hand, Luc reached through the bars to touch my chin and direct my eyes to his. The sparkle was still there and he didn't look as I had expected. "I knew you'd glamoured me, or something, this is far too intense for rational explanation."

"Luc, I swear to you, I have done nothing to you. I don't understand this either."

Luc smirked at me. "Jenna, I'm joking, no magic could fully explain how I feel when I'm with you. You have transfixed me. I see your face in my dreams and I miss you when we're apart. I feel like I have known you forever, even though we met less than three months ago. Considering that what you just told me should have me running for the hills in fear, I have never felt safer. If anything, I feel an irrational compulsion to follow you everywhere to make sure you're safe. I just don't know what to do with any of this. It's crazy! All of it! But I have been happier, and more confused, these past few months than at any other time in my life. I really think that if you hadn't been here, I might have completely lost my mind with this whole revelation thing."

"No, Luc! Don't you see? From what Ana implied, if I hadn't been here you might never have changed. This is all my fault somehow. You have been dragged into this world by force, because I couldn't take my own advice and stay away from you. I wanted to see you again, and selfishly, I looked for you. I should have known better and yet I still looked for you!" I was almost shouting by now, it seemed so obvious to me that I had clearly ruined Luc's life, and I felt completely wretched.

"Jenna, my whole life I have felt a need for something I

could not fulfil. A yearning to be somewhere or find someone that was 'out there' somewhere. I feel like I've found a home when I'm with you. I feel complete and I know that sounds bat-shit crazy and unreasonably quick, but there it is. I won't have you beating yourself up over something that was always going to happen."

"You're going to sit here and tell me you believe in the Fates now?" I asked

"How can I not? I am either dreaming, completely insane, or everything in that damn book is real and freedom of choice is just an illusion. I'd take the Fates over crazy most days, and if you're only a dream, well to be honest I'd rather not wake up anyway." He looked at me almost shyly then, perhaps wondering if he'd revealed too much. There was really nothing I wanted to do more in that moment than curl into his arms, and let him take charge, but there was still a bloody silver cage between us. So we found ourselves in a slightly awkward, natural silence that had we been an established couple might have been filled with a kiss or perhaps more. But we weren't a 'normal' couple, or an established couple, and of course there was the bloody silver cage, so for lack of anything more interesting to suggest, I reached for the book and waved it at him questioningly.

"Go on," Luc said. "How else are we going to occupy ourselves?" With that slightly more awkward pause, I opened the book again.

23

Fate

Foretold by The Fates

It is my duty as the recorder of prophesies to oversee the faithful translation and scribing of any and all prophesies that are believed to be truthful and authentic.

There are those beings in this world whose visions will never be questioned.

The Fates are such beings and never would I take it upon myself to disbelieve any prophesy or foresight offered by them. As such the following entries are faithful and precisely scripted words as related to the Watchers for recording.

We, the Watchers have made no edits to the presentation and offer no insight into the meaning of the

TRANSFIXED

words, we simply watch and record.
    Evelyn, The Eternal

When water and wind become one,
The darkness shall quake in fear.

When fire and earth combine,
The light will grow strong.

The light in the darkness will summon the storm,
Many will drown in the deluge.

Imbibed with the strength of the four,
The light and the darkness will stand tall.

The portal will open,
And they may return.

The transitory path is riddled with bumps

When light binds the darkness,
The ripples spread far.

The path in the light,
Leads from darkness to fire.

24

Unwelcome Visitors

Jenna

I felt the rising of the sun as I do every day, with a waning of my strength and an almost dreamlike awareness of the world. Often I wish that I could sleep the daylight hours away, but not today. Today I was thankful for the path I was on, wherever it would take me. I was rather certain now that my journey alone had come to its end, and therefore it may be advisable if I tried to move forward with some form of preparation. Preparing for 'The Storm' though would not be easy since we had no idea what to expect.

Luc, for his part, seemed to be taking everything now at face value, but I sensed a deeper turmoil, which I could completely understand. Everything he knew about the world in which he lived had just been flung out the window of a moving vehicle and crushed by an oncoming truck. Not just smashed either, but completely obliterated. We had talked last night about Luc's work with the fire service. He said he'd always had a bit of a hero complex as a child and had wanted to help the smaller children that were being bullied. He noted it was always the smaller children he looked after and joked that it was probably because he was scared of bullies his own size. He used to help during the holidays, reading to the elderly in the nursing home just around the corner from where he had lived with his mother at that time. Lillith had told Luc that his grandmother had died there, and I watched him struggle with the realization that this had been a lie, to further colour Luc's world so that he wouldn't ask too many questions.

With that small truth came the realization that Luc had figuratively mourned the passing of a fictitious woman; he had felt keenly the loss of a grandmother who had never, in fact, existed. All things considered, he was doing remarkably well, and so I was not at all surprised when, on hearing the magical lock click open, Luc was up off the bed and into the main basement even as I blinked.

"Can we go somewhere? I can't be in this house anymore. I need to get away to clear my head and think straight." Without hesitation, I told Luc I had a place we could base from for a bit. I had a panic room in both homes so I would think that should I need to, I could contain an alpha wolf.

We told Lillith that we were going and she nodded vaguely like she wanted to say something but was trying not to. We took the opportunity to run, before she let loose whatever further revelations were coming our way. Idly I wondered what Ana would think when she reappeared, but she'd been nowhere to be seen, and to be honest, she seemed to be such a stalker that she probably already knew. Really, I wanted to visit my cottage, I felt a distinct need for its isolation and protection, but I couldn't really explain why, until we got to my apartment in town.

I could see the door had been forced as I walked towards the room, and I slowed down considerably. My senses went into high alert, basically a fight or flight response, only now I was completely aware of Luc's every movement too as both a potential backup but also as Light to be protected. What I really wanted to do was leave, with Luc, immediately. However, to get to the bottom of it, then I would need to know what they wanted—whoever 'they' were. I really couldn't see any other options. Luc, however, was quite on form, usually I look out only for myself. It was very strange to be led by his confidence instead. Leaning his back to the wall, Luc reached his arm out to gently push the door further open, which allowed me to see through to the living room from my vantage point.

I could see destruction everywhere, and logic told me the vandals were long gone, but I could hear erratic breathing from somewhere inside. The smell of blood was in the air, I would guess from the look on Luc's face, he was also picking up these signs and that his inevitably heightened senses hadn't really made themselves known until now. I really didn't want a confrontation now, with Luc still discovering himself. So caution was my guide as I slipped into the living room to survey the damage. As Luc followed me through, my eyes came to rest upon one of the housekeeping staff, lying back against the base of the sofa, eyes closed with blood smeared across her face.

I could hear her heartbeat was strong and suspected her erratic breathing had more to do with the memories than the attack, which should make my job easier. As I reached for her face, I felt Luc's hand on my shoulder and I looked up into troubled questioning eyes. "I'm okay," I reassured him. "I own my choices, not the other way round." He nodded then and I touched the woman's face, I felt a warmth in my fingers as I probed the wound on her cheek to try and establish how bad it was. It didn't look or really feel particularly serious, and I suspected it was more that she'd bumped her head on the way down.

As I watched the cut across her face began to knit together as though it had never been, Luc gasped and I felt his hand on my shoulder clench. I moved back, suddenly aware that this might be a trap, this woman was clearly supernatural to heal in such a way. How could I have been so stupid?

We sat and watched for another minute, and the wound did not heal anymore but continued to ooze. Her heartbeat, which had pulsed stronger for a moment, settled back into its healthy but shallow rhythm and her erratic breathing returned. We frowned at each other, and Luc asked if I had been healing her, still frowning I shook my head and then stopped. Had I been? My fingers were still tingling where they had touched the woman's wound. "It's not something I have ever done before," I replied, looking to Luc for guidance.

"Touch her wound again, Jenna, I think it was you," he suggested.

"Don't be ridiculous, Luc, I bring death not life." He quirked an eyebrow, which told me we'd be debating this later, and I briefly revelled in how easy this seemed to be for us, how naturally we worked as a team. I couldn't bring myself to worry too much about it just now though, as Luc was taking me by my already blood-covered hand and leading me to reach out and touch the housekeeper again.

He prompted me to touch her face, and as soon as I did, I felt the warmth return to my fingers and her wound again began to knit together. This time though, since I was paying more attention I suppose, I felt a drawing of energy not just from me, but from Luc, too, through the hand he still had on my arm. Looking down, I became aware of the glow emanating from the place where we touched. I looked to Luc and found him also staring at his hand on me, then as one we turned to the housekeeper as she groaned and her eyes began to flutter open. I held my hand to her face long enough to watch the wound close completely, before moving back to allow her some personal space.

As her eyes fluttered open, they still seemed glazed and unfocussed, for a moment, before casting over the chaotic mess that was my living room and finally settling on me. "Miss Genevieve, I'm so sorry." She struggled to sit up and I quickly reassured her it was okay to stay unmoving for the time being.

"Can you tell me what has happened here?" I asked, glancing around to signify the room and chaos, not the fact that she was asleep on my floor.

Slowly she explained that she had been here emptying the bins and cleaning when the door was broken open. She told us that the 'devil men' had come and they were shouting at her, that they were looking for 'the pendant' that was what they had called it. Even when they had discovered my jewellery in the next room, they had not been satisfied. They had wanted Carla, as we discovered the young lady was named, to tell them where I was and when would I be back. Did I spend my days here? This seemingly vague information told me much, and although she'd been hurt, I was glad for the information I had gleaned from Carla. When she felt steadier, I sent her on her way, with instructions to be seen by the doctor who lived downstairs. He was a private practitioner, but I assured Carla that I would pay the bill since she had been hurt in my home.

Luc started to make moves toward tidying up and I held his hand to stop him. "Leave it, Luc, I'll have someone come in and do it. There is nothing important kept here, it's just slightly more convenient than my actual home." It occurred to me then that maybe I should check the panic room and walked through to the bedroom where the walk-in cupboard lay open, with its contents strewn everywhere. I reached up for the secret button that was not only high but also behind a lip and low enough to be missed by searching fingers. I had to step over a pile of clothes and shoes to enter, so I was fairly certain that no one was inside but had better check anyway, and of course I could roll back my CCTV while I was here. There was no audio, which made Carla's revelation all the more important but maybe I knew the idiots. She'd described them as devil men with red eyes, so they were likely vampire. Heads would roll when I got to the bottom of this.

After we left the apartment, we headed towards the outskirts of town on foot. We had rolled the CCTV back, and unsurprisingly I spotted Anthony lingering in the doorway whilst his lackeys trashed my home. I guess he was hoping to go unnoticed since his involvement would directly implicate Marcus. Especially since I knew Anthony—and as such, Marcus—hadn't known about the place prior to Anthony following me there a few months before.

"Can you all do that?" Luc asked, pulling me from my

murderous thoughts

"Do what?" I replied

"Heal people, with your touch…?"

"Can all humans sing?" I asked sarcastically in response.

Luc's completely straight-faced answer was, "Well, now that really depends on A: How good the acoustics are in your shower and B: how much alcohol has been consumed…" I couldn't help but laugh and there it was, murderous rage dissipated, just like that. WTF?

"So…Can you?" Luc prompted, and I looked across to see genuine intrigue where I was fully expecting to see horror, rejection, or any number of negative responses to my general weirdness.

"Ah, no! Not that I'm aware of anyway. That's not something I have personally ever experienced before." He nodded as though this confirmed something for him.

"And do you think that had something to do with me?" he asked next. I stopped walking; we looked at each other for a moment while I considered my words carefully.

"Luc, I think you have a huge learning curve ahead, and I suspect your changes are still coming. But it may well have something to do with it and maybe we should explore that more, at some point." Again Luc just nodded and started walking again. I followed him quietly, letting him think it through whilst I considered what to do about Marcus' invasion into my space.

It smacked of desperation to me. I wondered what had changed, and then glancing towards Luc, I thought I might know the answer to that. That however would assume intelligence of some sort on Marcus' side and also intent beyond simply subverting my will for vain reasons. He was clearly having me followed if he knew about Luc, which meant Lillith and Ana may also be within the target now. We would need to tell them I decided and increased my pace just slightly.

Luc obviously noticed and frowned at me. "I think that we should perhaps speak with Ana and your mother, just to make sure they are aware someone trashed my home. I'm thinking that it may have something to do with the time I have spent with you. I have almost certainly been followed, but the question is to where exactly, and for how long. I can't even tell you how much that disturbs me, that someone could track me without my knowing."

Luc stopped again and took my hands. "Okay, I think you may be right. We should head back to Mum's, but I don't want to stay there. I need to be able to think and move and not feel so under scrutiny all the time. Can we find somewhere else?" I reassured him that the apartment hadn't been our final destination anyway and that the cottage was most definitely secure.

When we arrived at Lillith's home it was to find Ana had yet to return, although I spotted a large black crow watching from the tree opposite and studiously ignored it, whilst thinking, 'Is that you?' The crow cawed loudly as though in response, and I decided that it was indeed Ana, maybe she could feel the eyes, too? 'Be aware, Ana, enemies watching,' I thought to her and again the crow cawed loudly. I decided it was definitely Ana and told her to pay attention to the conversation in the house.

We entered and found Lillith in the living room, looking through the book. She looked up and immediately stood. "What has happened?" she asked quickly. We explained all we had learned, and she was already moving as we finished with the fact that the intruders were looking for a pendant of some kind. Lillith thrust the book into my arms. "Guard this with your life and learn it, both of you. All of our lives will soon depend upon it. You have somewhere to go, Jenna?" she asked me

"Yes, of course, it's very safe." She nodded and summoned Luc to accompany her, whilst I kept a watch out. I could see nothing when I looked out but I could feel the eyes on me. I wondered if they were Ana's eyes or someone else's.

When Luc returned he was carrying two bags and a look of mild shock, but he said nothing other than, "Put the book in here," whilst thrusting one of the bags towards me.

Lillith returned with a Bible, of all things, clutched in her hands, which she opened to reveal a carved out centre full of cash. Half of this she gave to Luc, and the other half she tucked into a hidden pocket in her skirts. "Everything is in the bag?" she asked Luc and he nodded. She placed her hand on our bag then, and it transformed immediately into a packet of sweetie looking little things in a clear box type packet with a flip lid. She flicked the lid open and it changed back into a bag, closed the lid, and it was sweets again. She did all this without a single word and I realized she did not want to be overheard. She then changed her own bag into a shopping basket that fitted the look she presented. "Well," Lillith said out loud, "I need to go to the shop. You two enjoy your hotel stay, I booked it under Smith." She laughed then and handed Luc a piece of paper that was clearly handwritten. "Here is your booking confirmation and please give Cousin Grace a hug from me when you see her." With that Lillith swept out the door and was gone. We looked together at the letter she'd given to Luc.

Luc and Jenna,

This has come quicker than I had expected, so please forgive me for the rather rushed way we are parting. I will be fine and making my own preparations and so must you. As I said, LEARN the book, you will need to know and quite possibly use everything that can be learned from it in the coming storm, and you must remain strong and together.

From here you should take the train to Cambridge. I have kept a house there that is fully maintained and the paper trail suggests it belongs to my 'fictitious' cousin, Grace

Kennedy. That should lead any followers a merry chase, just long enough for you to disappear. Do <u>Not</u> go to Grace Kennedy's house, it is warded and a danger to anyone that tries to enter. From the station in Cambridge, I trust you can disappear successfully and make your way to wherever Jenna hides.

Jenna - Please look after my boy, he's the only thing that really matters to me in this world.

When it's time we will come together again, but until then there will be no point looking for me. I shall change my appearance once lost in the crowd and then I will go to ground.

Take care—both of you and remember—You are stronger together and sometimes the heart must lead the head, not the other way around.

My Love,

Lillith

Luc and I looked at each other and nodded silently. Luc pocketed the sweetie box and the letter and we left the house. We strolled as casually as we could through town and towards the train station, where we made quite a show of buying tickets for and boarding the train to Cambridge, which we had absolutely no intention of ever reaching.

———

Ana watched Luc and Jenna until they were safely

installed on the train. She continued to watch as Marcus' henchmen discovered that the train was headed to Cambridge. She listened to their plans and discovered that their enquiries had uncovered one Grace Kennedy, whom was a cousin to Luc's mother, Lillith, and owned a house in Cambridge. She would have smiled when they decided that Luc and Jenna were clearly headed for that address, except she was still a crow and could not.

Satisfied that all was going to plan, for the moment, she flew off into the distance to set more plans into action.

25

Self Discovery

Jenna

The train journey was tedious as long train journeys usually are. We spoke of nothing important in this most public of places and passed the time simply enjoying each other's view of the world, as it related to the superficial. We passed through a small village station at some point, and with a look and a nod, we decided without words to disembark. We moved unassumingly through the station, remaining at all times aware for any sign of somebody following. The village was small and we rented a room at the pub for the night. We paid cash and kept to ourselves. I suggested to the landlady that we might be newlyweds and this afforded a fair amount of privacy, without seeming to be deliberately hiding. The time passed without event, and we had a walk outside to familiarise ourselves with the area 'just in case.'

As luck would have it, there was open parkland opposite with a footpath that led straight into what looked to be a fair-sized forest. We could easily disappear here I decided, but the question I now had was how to travel. Alone I could simply run, and even at this distance, it wouldn't take long, but Luc's abilities were still developing and we had no idea of his current stamina. I guess it was time to start discovering what he could do.

I suggested to Luc that we head into the forest for a bit of an experiment, and he readily agree so we meandered off in that direction. Once we'd drifted a few hundred metres beyond the tree line, we left the path and broke into the forest proper. Once we felt safe and secluded, we stopped and Luc asked what I had in mind.

"So, I think you'll find that your strength and speed will have increased some since your change, and I am thinking it's a good idea if you know your limits before we head into any kind of trouble. So I thought maybe if we start with strength? I'll make a fist and you try to push it back with the one hand."

Luc looked at me quite incredulously that I should assume he couldn't push me back, but he agreed anyway and we faced each other. I lifted my right hand and made a fist, he lifted his hand and wrapped it around mine. "Okay," I said "On three, one...two...three."

I pressed forward slightly, and then gradually increased the pressure, Luc's look was quite smug to begin with, but predictably as I began to push rather than just hold my fist up, Luc began to frown. He moved his feet so they were braced better, and then he also began leaning into my hand, which tempted me beyond words to just pull my hand away. I resisted though and again increased my pressure to test him further. He was shooting me looks now that belied his calm exterior, and I knew he was doubting now if he could hold me back, should I try to actually hit him.

Knowing that I was still only using a fraction of my own strength, and that he was starting to struggle a bit, I increased once more. I felt Luc start to slip, his eyes shot to mine and I offered him a smile; he frowned in response and leaned even more into my hand. I tried to resist, I really did, but the temptation was just too much for me. I released the pressure I was applying and Luc fell, stumbling forward into my space. I steadied him as he caught his balance, his scowl at me made the whole thing even more amusing to me, and I was not far off giggling. Luc made a show of brushing imaginary lint from his shirt and passed comment about not wanting to make me feel bad. He looked very sheepish in that moment, and I once again, felt that strange, flip and flutter in my stomach area. This was new ground for me, never before had I gotten to know anyone well enough to have experienced any kind of emotional attachment. I wasn't sure that I liked it. I was also entirely unconvinced that I didn't like it.

Luc seemed to realize I was having a moment and reached out to squeeze my hand before stepping back. "So, speed then...?" he asked, looking around.

Focus on something else Jenna, fantastic idea. "Race you to the lake!" I shouted and was gone. I heard him curse behind me and set off in chase. I reached the lake within seconds and had scaled a nearby tree before I heard him catching up. He arrived at the lake edge at least thirty seconds behind me, and I wondered if that was because he was actually slower or because he still thought he was.

I was feeling particularly playful today and dropped down silently behind him, so close I could feel his body heat pressing against my coldness. I whispered, "Boo," into his ear, and then laughed out loud as he spun, stumbled, and fell unceremoniously on his arse.

He scowled at my proffered hand and climbed to his feet. I could see the questions behind his eyes but he seemed to be tallying them up at the moment so I didn't push. Moving on, I asked, "Do you know how to fight, Luc?"

"I am not a scrapper, if that's what you mean, but I could probably defend myself." He stood slightly straighter with that last comment. I felt a bit sorry that I would have to bruise his ego, but potentially his life might depend on what I could teach him about fighting vampires and so, ego aside, this had to be done.

"Okay, as you've seen I am fast and very strong. From

what little I know about werewolves, they are stronger and faster in human form than a regular human, but as a wolf they have strength and speed enough to take down a vampire—if they're lucky. That, of course, is assuming that the myths I have heard have any truth to them at all. So either way, we need to know, and so I challenge you to defend yourself against me. What do you think?"

He looked at me for a moment in silence before asking, "You want me to fight you?"

I smiled. "You can try, if you like. I really don't think you'll land a hit on me, what I asked you to do was defend yourself. Can you stop me from landing a hit on you? Ready?" He nodded slowly and dropped back into a vague fighting stance. I could tell immediately he'd never been in a fight that was expected; possibly not even an unexpected confrontation, and I had to wonder again at his courage that night in the alley, when he tried to save me from my meal.

I began to pace him, circling around just out of range and making the odd darting movement. I didn't want to throw him in at the deep end by going for him with force, but I didn't want to go easy and have him underestimate what a vampire could do. Marcus had marked us as a target, we would be coming up against some of the most ruthless and battle-hardened vamps that money could buy. The idiots worked for blood and gold, in other words. Greedy idiots with absolutely no sense of moral compass. Not that vampires were well known for their moral compass of course, but some were definitely better than others.

We continued to circle each other, and I watched the way Luc was moving. He looked mostly awkward and unsure, he was watching me warily and attempting to predict my moves. I struck out and got a touch on his right bicep, his frown told me that I had surprised him. I got another three touches in before he managed to block one. His moves were growing smoother, and I felt that I could now feel his wolf pacing just below the surface. Every now and then, I would see a glint in those beautiful eyes that was pure animal.

My monster too was pacing, she wanted out to play, but I kept her below the surface. Luc was doing really well, taking in all this new information and rolling with it, but I didn't want to terrify him by introducing her too soon. If Ana was right, then it wouldn't matter to him, but I still didn't want to take the chance of losing him just yet. Deciding it was time to step it up, I flashed behind him and wrapped my arm around his neck. Before I could get a good hold though, he'd twisted away and out of reach. I smiled and raised an eyebrow, impressed.

He was definitely growing into himself the longer we played this game, so I kept pushing. I would circle and tag him, circle back and tag him again. Never hard, I didn't want to hurt him, but he needed to understand us and how we could move. After fifteen minutes or so, he held up his hand and as I straightened, he pulled off the shirt he'd been wearing. I tried not to look, but... just...Oh! Where the hell did he get that body? I wanted to know. I realized that actually he'd changed a lot physically since we'd met. He'd been fairly slight of build that first night, but now he was looking more broad shouldered and...well...buff, really. I was a little surprised by this observation, and was clearly staring like a fool, because suddenly he chuckled almost self-consciously and asked if I was enjoying the view.

Now that it was my turn to be self-conscious, I mumbled slightly and couldn't fathom a witty response so instead I flashed out my hand and smacked him on the arm. "Come on, no rest for the wicked." We started circling again while he smirked at me. I slowly pushed him harder, and after about another thirty minutes, he was beginning to tire mentally from constantly trying to second-guess me. I could almost see his wolf pacing behind his eyes, and I wondered what Luc was doing to hold him back, and whether he even knew he was doing it.

I could just feel there was so much more power there than we had tapped so far, but I wasn't quite sure how to trigger him, besides getting angry at someone. I sped up a little more, and suddenly I felt the change ripple through the air; it felt almost like an electric charge through the atmosphere. I was just moving towards Luc, intending to tackle him down, and suddenly his wolf was in my face. In an explosion of shredded material I found myself unexpectedly on my back with an alpha wolf pinning me down. He growled into my exposed throat, and I thought for a second that I had pushed too far and his wolf would end me.

Then his eyes met mine. I could only imagine they must looked panicked in this moment, and then he gave me a look that could only be a grin. He promptly laid himself down on top of me and started licking my face. It was really quite disgusting, and I shrieked with laughter, trying to bat him away. Suddenly magic rippled outward from him again, and instead of being pinned by his big beautiful wolf; I found myself looking into a pair of gorgeous and shocked blue eyes, with a rather naked and embarrassed Luc pinning me still to the forest floor. As he changed, the pendant I hadn't noticed him wearing before, dropped into my face and caught my attention. Luc started to stammer an awkward apology but the pendant had completely transfixed me, and I reached out for it, but stopped at the last second. It too seemed imbued with magic and I was suddenly hesitant to touch something that seemed somehow defensive.

I decided to try and put it out of my mind and instead deal with the somewhat awkward situation we'd found ourselves in. "So, Lugus. Tell me the truth; this was secretly your plan all along, wasn't it? Get me alone and trusting you and then simply throw off your clothes and force me to admire you?"

He chuckled and again tried to apologise as I tried to get up, inadvertently making matters worse. "Jenna, please," he said somewhat breathlessly, confusing me. I suddenly realized what the problem was and froze. Having always felt disparity for others of my kind and never being of a mind to play with my food, I had never had a physical relationship with another. I knew, of course, how it all worked in theory but had never partaken myself.

As Luc struggled to get his rather obvious arousal under control, I realized that the fluttery, flip feelings I sometimes had when I was with Luc, and that were threatening to make my head swim now, were quite likely my own attraction to him, and being unexperienced I simply hadn't known. This realization did nothing to help the situation, of course, as he closed his eyes and tried to think of anything else. My own breathing was spiky and erratic now, and I struggled mentally with the simultaneous desires to flee and reach up and claim his lips.

They looked to be soft and yielding and I wanted to know how he tasted. I wanted to claim him and have him be mine, and I suddenly didn't care a bit if that was right or wrong. I didn't care that I had chosen not to play in the Light. I wanted to bath in Luc's light and goodness. I felt suddenly desperate to never be parted from him; I felt that my survival depended upon him in some fundamental way. I was just coming to the conclusion that I might just be reckless enough to kiss him when his eyes opened suddenly and looked deep into mine. We both froze and something just clicked for me then, it seemed so natural to be here, with him. It seemed to me then like time stretched and that this single moment was in fact eternal.

We stared at each other a moment longer, and then with a tortured groan, Luc rolled away and sat with his back to me, hunched over into himself. I continued to lay there taking deep, unnecessary breaths and wrestling with my composure, painfully aware of Luc sitting right next to me doing exactly the same. Eventually we got it under control, and Luc reached for the top he had shed what felt like hours ago. "Did you have the sweetie box, bag with you?" I asked. He confirmed it had been in his trouser pocket, so I started to search around for where it may have gone when he had burst out of his clothes so spectacularly.

26

Binding

Jenna

When Luc was finally dressed again, he still looked really awkward and embarrassed. I thought I had best help him deal with it. "So, it would seem your wolf is definitely stronger and faster physically than your man. I guess we need to work out how to call him when you want rather than when he decides he's ready." Luc looked at me with an expression similar to a drowning man thrown a lifeline. He clearly had no idea how to deal with what had happened, and so my offer to talk around it was gratefully received. He also used it to throw out the apology he obviously had stuck in his throat.

"I don't really know what happened there, it was like I

just wasn't me, but I was. I was there but not in charge. I don't suppose that makes any sense, does it? I'm sorry, Jenna." He looked up at me then with hope and shame simultaneously in his eyes and on his face. I just smiled and took his hand, squeezing his fingers. I was dealing with my own confusion about how it had made me feel. The simple fact that I had felt something physically was in itself an overwhelming revelation, and I needed time to think. So we awkwardly stumbled around the subject like teenagers on a first date and surrounded by onlookers.

"Actually," I started, "I do kind of understand that, let me tell you about my monster. Maybe that will help."

"Your monster?" Luc asked looking confused.

"Yes, that's how it feels and I keep her on a very tight lead. She is the side of me that is written about in vampire books and visualised in films. She is evil incarnate and she shares this body with me. She requires feeding with blood, and only blood, and as long as I feed her, I am granted immortal life, amazing strength, and super speed. There are other things that I can do, but I am starting to realize that these 'extras' are possibly due to my parentage and not my monster."

"Does she have a name? Or do you simply call her Monster?" Luc asked

"Our given name is Genevieve as I told you, and that is how I think of her. She is Genevieve, The Woman of the Race, The White Wave."

"What does that mean?" Luc wanted to know

"I don't really know, this I am told is the meaning of our name. Long ago though, I chose to become Jenna. Genevieve requires blood to survive, and she cares not where it comes from, or that another must lose their life to attain it. Jenna, however, does care, I became very concerned with the loss of innocent life in order to sustain my existence, and I made a choice. I decided that with my gifts I could easily choose only to take from the Darkness. I could prey upon the predators within human society and make the world a little lighter, one night at a time. In this way, we came to have peace between us. She still gets fed her food of choice, and my conscience is a little lighter."

"When you say food of choice...?"

"Human blood, we need blood to survive and its consumption is vital. I could survive indeterminately for example upon the blood of rats or fish, however it is vile and the experience is vastly different. It lacks depth and satisfaction; I imagine this is similar to surviving from McDonald's foods scraps out of the bin, or having the money for fillet mignon every night. Human blood is what we need to remain in optimum condition and at top strength."

"Okay, and you said you have other gifts? Are they too, gifts from Genevieve?"

"Well, actually, I don't know, I have no long-term memories to fall back on. I am older than even I am aware, Luc, and my memories prior to the last few centuries are hazy at best and non-existent at worst. I simply do not know who I was then, but I know I existed."

While I was talking, Luc had moved around behind me to lean against a tree, and he pulled me gently back now until I was sitting, not on his lap but between his legs with my back against his chest. He felt so warm to me and I greedily revelled in his heat. I was glad the wall had disappeared again and snuggled back into him, this seemed to encourage him and his arms snaked around me.

I felt so safe right here. We were sitting on the ground in the middle of woodland I didn't know the name of, whilst on the run from unknown enemies, and preparing for a fight, but in that moment I could not have felt safer or more cared for, and that was a completely alien concept to me.

"I know who you are," Luc stated confidently when we'd settled

"You do?"

"Yes, you're beautiful, strong, and you've chosen a difficult path. You've chosen to be more than the universe says you should be, and although you doubt yourself, you remain strong enough to follow your chosen ideals, even though I suspect it would be easier to just give in to temptation.

"I find myself wanting to protect you, even though you could probably kill me in a second. I want to be with you because you inspire me to be more, and you always have, even before I knew any of this. There is something about you that calls to me, and I...I simply can't ignore it." I had turned in his arms to look at him while he was talking. Again I wanted to steal a kiss, this lovely, light individual had just offered me his heart, and I so wanted to take it and make it mine. I wanted to keep him with me forever. My logical brain was screaming not to do this, don't get involved, he's Light and I must not extinguish his flame. My heart currently felt like it might actually be beating normally, and it ached. It wanted to love and be allowed to connect with another. I was so conflicted that I simply froze, twisted in his arms, and ensnared by his eyes that looked straight into me and saw the lost soul that hides inside this cold shell.

I could see the same conflict and need in his face, and then I wasn't thinking anymore. He'd leaned forward ever so slightly and I closed the gap. When his lips touched mine for that very first time, it felt like time had stopped. It felt to me as though something inside of me had unlocked, and that untold power had flooded our bodies and the world, as we chose to be together. I felt light and infinitely powerful at the same time as I took his face in my hands and twisted so we were facing each other. His hand snaked up into my hair and held me fast. I don't think I could have pulled away if I'd wanted to, and we remained that way for some time.

Eventually the intensity passed and I felt now hollow but deeply fulfilled. At some point, I had changed my position so that I was straddling Luc, and we stayed like that, for a long time. My head rested on his shoulder and he ran his hands through my hair. We were alert to the sounds of the forest but still I felt utterly at peace and safe here. Sometime later, Luc started to doze and we lay together on the forest floor. He slept in my arms that night and I knew that something had changed. I felt now that our life force ebbed and flowed as one rather than in tandem. It felt as though that one single kiss had changed our fate or path, or perhaps just sealed us onto it. I imagined that if I called out for Ana, she might be able to explain all this to me, but I wanted to be in nobody else's company but Luc's right now. So I held my questions and watched him sleep peacefully, with his arm flung casually across my waist. I might possibly have had a few thoughts about what else might follow from our first kiss, but in that respect the promise of the night remained unfulfilled.

27

Ripples

Ana

I watched them training in the forest during the late afternoon. Jenna again had no idea that I was here, and I had kept silent so as not to alert her. I was glad to see they were experimenting with Luc's new abilities and that Jenna seemed to be thinking along the right lines. I didn't think it would be long before they bonded permanently, but even I was shocked when it was this day.

They'd had an awkward moment when Luc's wolf had introduced himself to Jenna, leaving Luc embarrassingly naked and sprawled across her, but they'd gotten over their mutual embarrassment. Even from this distance, I could see the attraction they both felt was right there on the surface, almost like a palpable thing that wanted attention. Jenna told him about herself, opening up to the first person ever in her long, long life.

When he opened up to her, it was like someone had flicked a switch under her skin, she seemed to light up from within, and I almost began to worry until they kissed. It was like they had moved outside of time, as fate took over and bonded them forever.

In choosing each other as mates, Jenna's immortal life would now be shared and neither would age another moment. Luc would quickly continue through his transformation now unhindered by mortality, and the door had been kicked wide open for Jenna's transformation to begin in earnest. It was foretold that once they came together, they would grow to be an unstoppable force, and that with their combined abilities they would have the power to lead the supernatural world in either peace or war. Personally, I was hoping for war, but the die was cast, and it was up to Jenna and Luc now.

The powerful shockwaves of their binding rippled outward and were likely felt in all corners of the earth, to some extent. Luc slept peacefully now in Jenna's arms, and I could well imagine how her thoughts might look tonight, but I stayed out of her head. Things were moving along well, and so I felt no need to interfere right now. Let them enjoy their peace while they could. I had no doubt I would soon be summoned for questioning, I could wait until then.

Spreading my wings, I flew upwards and out of the forest.

Lillith

The shockwave struck my heart and affected me as it would no else but Luc and Jenna. My mortality was tied to Luc's, and as he was bound to Jenna and joined the supernatural world in earnest. So my voluntary mortality was stripped from me, and I was restored once more to my full power and strength, well eventually. I would have to practice to regain my control, but the ability was restored and oh, how I had missed it. The storm was truly coming now, it was time to prepare.

Marcus

Something was wrong, I felt a shockwave ripple through the very fabric of space and time, and it concerned me deeply. I felt that, in that moment, my place had been threatened. There is nothing I would not do to secure my place in this world, and I must discover what this new threat might be. Fate seemed to be moving on the winds and I liked it not.

"Henry!" I bellowed into the room at large, the useless idiot's hearing was good enough that he would hear me wherever he may be in the chateau.

"Sir! How may I serve you?"

"Did you feel that, Henry? There is strong magic on the winds, and I want to know what is happening, go to the Fates and demand that they tell you!" Henry looked as though I had asked him to cut his balls off and eat them. I was pacing now, I felt as restless as a caged lion and I needed to do something.

"Sir, the Fates do not usually respond well to demands and orders. They may however acquiesce to your request for some small token of your esteem. A bauble or trinket of some kind?" Henry suggested. I waved my hand casually towards the table. It would certainly be a small price to pay for the information I decided as I stalked from the room.

Henry

I felt the shockwave ripple through the chateau and almost instantly I was summoned. "Henry!" Marcus bellowed from his study, so of course I rushed to do my master's bidding.

"Sir! How may I serve you?"

"Did you feel that, Henry? There is strong magic on the winds, and I want to know what is happening, go to the Fates and demand that they tell you!" Marcus demanded pacing like a lion in a zoo.

"Sir, the Fates do not usually respond well to demands and orders. They may however acquiesce to your request for some small token of your esteem. A bauble or trinket of some kind?" I suggested carefully. I could see the tension in Marcus and knew only too well the consequences of angering him, unfortunately the time had not yet come to reveal myself, so I would remain calm and cool as only Henry could, under such pressure. Marcus spared me barely a glance and flicked his hand vaguely towards the box on the table.

"Yes, fine, take them a gift, whichever you think." With that he stalked from the office, looking for someone to punish and I smiled to myself. I removed the ring I would need from the box and closed the lid. I placed the ring in a velvet bag from the desk and tucked it into my inside left pocket—the secret one. Patting my right breast to double check the contents of the other pocket, I then dressed for the cold. Visiting the Fates was for most, a 'fate' worse than death, but for me; you could say it was a little like going home.

―――

Somewhere in the depths of the forest, an ancient wolf awoke from a long and tortured sleep.

―――

The Lady Camilla opened her eyes for the first time in years. She did not sleep but when she lay very still, she could almost believe that she dreamed. Something though was different, some spike of power or knowledge disturbed her rest. The Fates felt restless, as though change were coming, some kind of storm. Camilla tried to ignore the ache, it was an ancient and gnawing guilt for the child she had failed to raise. She denied to herself that she had cared for the child;

it was best that she died or she might have threatened Camilla's reign. She did miss the girl terribly though.

Epilogue

Fated Choices

The Fates

Henry

The Fates are as fickle as they are gruesome to behold, unfortunately our paths cross often, and I am forced to endure their eccentric ramblings

This day is no different, although they seem even more frenzied than is usual.

Wittering on about choice and fate being intertwined and inseparable.

Apparently all paths are fated but not all are chosen.

The crones inform me again, that all outcomes can be foretold but choice presents all manner of hurdles for the seer.

Eventual destinations, they assure me, are usually the same, but the path can vary greatly because of choice.

They seem to forget that I am in fact very familiar with this concept of choice shaping fate and derailing even the best laid plans.

"Hag! Cease your incessant mumblings and speak plain with me! What has happened this day?" I bellow upon entering the chamber and being pointedly ignored at first. Justine turned her unseeing face towards me in an instant, scowling her displeasure, which I can assure you looks quite alarming when the scowler has no eyes. She stalked forward, unerringly, to where I stood and faced me head on. "You would speak to me thus, and yet you still expect obedience and truth? Where are your manners, boy?" Truly, only Justine would dare to offer me such disrespect and fully expect me to simply accept it. Of course, I am the only being that could survive calling the sisters hags and expect to walk away with my head still attached. Fortune- tellers they may be, but they are also colder than the pure blue heart of Ice Mountain. Justine sniffed haughtily and turned back towards her sisters. Sophia looked me over and then held out her hand expectantly, I smiled at her and handed over the velvet bag from my right hand breast pocket.

Sophia looked at me a moment longer and then chose to say nothing other than, "You come for news?" to which I nodded my ascent. Sophia had no use for my words, since she was unable to hear them, but she always knew why you had come. I had never known her be wrong in all the time I had known her. Sometimes she would tell you, why you had come and the reason you had thought it was otherwise. With no further ado, she tossed the bag I had given her into the bubbling pot on the stove. Sophia and her sisters set about adding dried bits of twig and what smelled like a variety of herbs that could be found in most kitchens.

I turned away though, as Justine added something from a jar that sloshed ominously. My eyes strayed to the third sister as Justine and Sophia started their chanting and calling nonsense. Saffron, being mute, had no part to play in the speaking of words, and so her contribution was silent and magical to behold. She moved with the grace of a dancer in a manner that truly belied her age and looks. Here, in movement, you could see through the façade to the maiden she truly was. Why she followed her sisters in their hideous guise I had never decided, but follow she did, only here within her spell work dance could one glimpse the truly beautiful soul trapped within.

As the vocalization increased in pitch and fervour, so smoke began to plume from the pot. Initially it was fairly standard in appearance, but slowly began to thicken and swirl, there was a brightness growing from within that seemed purple and pulsing, and suddenly Jenna stepped from the smoke, followed closely by a large white and grey wolf.

She seemed to me, different, somehow. The way she

held herself more confident, almost regal, you could say. The wolf seemed to be her ally, and as he approached, she laid a gentle but proprietary hand upon his shoulder, almost like a lover offering comfort and reassurance. I frowned at this image, unsure of its meaning until the wolf imagery swirled into chaos and was suddenly replaced with that of a young man. His dark blond hair and sparkling blue eyes drew my attention, and I noted the devotion with which he gazed upon Jenna and then took her hand.

This must be the chosen mate, he certainly seemed devoted enough, and if he was a wolf shifter, then he would be strong and fast enough to keep pace with Jenna, these were good things for the coming trials. I felt more at ease then as it became clear to me that Jenna and her chosen mate had clearly bonded deeply. This I deduced must be have been the catalyst for the ripples of power that had so affected 'my master.'

Marcus was such a pompous and intolerable fool. I felt a deep aversion to the man, and it was all I could do to wait patiently as my daughter and her chosen mate travelled their path at an almost leisurely pace. It would certainly be my great honour to help overthrow Marcus when the time came.

After Word

Truly, writing Transfixed has been awesome and the next chapter is already in the works. If you'd like to be informed first about my current projects then you can sign up to my newsletter here:

Sign Up Here :-D

I promise here and now, to never spam you with randomness– well maybe a little but only tiny amounts of sparkly randomness.

Alternatively my social media hangouts are:

Facebook

Twitter

And Wordpress